PARANOISIA

PARANOISIA

Oliver Charles Gearing

Matador
9 Priory Business Park,
Wistow Road, Kibworth Beauchamp,
Leicestershire. LE8 0RX
Tel: (+44) 116 279 2299
Fax: (+44) 116 279 2277
Email: books@troubador.co.uk
Web: www.troubador.co.uk/matador

ISBN 9781780883731

British Library Cataloguing in Publication Data.
A catalogue record for this book is available from the British Library.

Typeset by Troubador Publishing Ltd, Leicester, UK
Printed and bound in Great Britain by TJ International Ltd, Padstow, Cornwall

Matador is an imprint of Troubador Publishing Ltd

For my family, who supported me through the story,
and the book that followed

In a bleak, sound-proofed room, a tall, somewhat effeminate man sits on a steel-fixed chair staring at a mirrored wall, the small square tiles shining with a clinical cleanliness. His green eyes swivel about in his head, looking for something of interest. A man in a chcap white shirt and chino trousers steps in through a security door with a clipboard; he taps his way over to the table in worn leather shoes, pulling a biro from his shirt pocket and sits opposite the mysterious gentleman.

Artificial air hangs heavy in the room, with a deep cold from lack of heat over a long period of time.

'What are your experiences in general with hypnotism?' the man with the biro asks.

'I have been a professional hypnotist for at least fifteen years,' the smartly-dressed man replies. 'At present, I am employed on a very confidential basis two days a week.'

'Can you obtain information from an individual, willing or unwilling, by hypnotism?'

'Definitely, yes. Many of the medical cases I work on involve obtaining personal, intimate information and, through hypnotism, I have been quite successful in

1

obtaining this. If an individual refuses to co-operate with hypnosis, the doctors with whom I work use drugs, always sodium amytal.'

'Have you ever had any experience with drugs?'

'Yes, many times. I have worked with doctors using sodium amytal and Pentothal and have obtained hypnotic control after the drugs were used. In fact, many times drugs were used for the purpose of obtaining hypnotic control.'

'Have you ever wondered whether hypnotism could be used as a weapon?'

'Yes, I have thought about this often. It could certainly be used in obtaining information from recalcitrant people, particularly with drugs. It could be used as a recruiting source for special types of work. A good hypnotist running hypnotic shows for entertainment would pick up a great many subjects, some of whom might be exceptionally good subjects for us. These subjects could easily be tabbed and put to use.'

'Can individuals be made to do things under hypnosis that they would not otherwise?'

The effeminate man smiles and taps a row of fingers on the desk. The man with the biro looks at him blankly, waiting for a response. He eventually coughs in irritation to prompt him.

'Individuals could be taught to do anything, including murder, suicide, etc. I do believe that you could carry out acts that would be against an individual's moral feelings if they were psychologically conditioned.'

★ ★ ★

'In the ages of the rude beginning of culture, man believed that he was discovering a second real world in dream, and here is the origin of all metaphysics. Without dreams, mankind would never have had occasion to invent such a division of the world. The parting of soul and body goes also with this way of interpreting dreams; likewise, the idea of a soul's apparitional body: whence all belief in ghosts, and apparently, too, in gods.'
(Nietzsche)

I was filled with anger as a result of the monotonous days filled with the familiar faces of terrible people. London was full of the energy-sucking hate and putrid architecture of the criminal drug world. It seemed to me that, for every evening I spent chasing rainbows with the undesirable elements of the city, I became more aware of how much I loathed myself and the desire for the 'true' high became a dangerous polar opposite.

As Austin lifted the rusty spoon within eye line of the room, he flicked the lighter into action. The lack of conversation between him and I provided the perfect background for the sour bubbles. This was a Tuesday and, despite the silence of the apartment, the world I was living in was distinctively noisy.

Austin was six feet tall and balding. While the odd stray hair would bounce into view in good light, it was his portly stomach that hit the eyes. When he made an attempt to head into the outside world, perhaps to 'pick up' or buy convenience food, he moved like a sloth with vigor in his eyes. A man glued to his own decay. To me, he smelt of old cigarettes and cheap food, but the longer you spent around him, the less you were inclined to notice.

Austin stood up, having completed his small stash of drugs, and eyeballed his old, sticky phone. The clothes were badly matched and worn for comfort. The dark colours and ancient, wooly hat blended with the murky paths and streets of the city. When he could make the effort to speak, the words were strained and gargled as a result of smoke-inhaled, broken-down lungs.

'I can get something now from round the gardens.'

His eyes were constantly narrowed, with the look of someone permanently in shock. Women often averted their gaze, as any eye contact caused him to produce a creepy smirk and a broken cough. Enough to put you off your morning coffee at least.

The quality of the drugs was awful. If you were to buy local, and the dealers know you're local, then inevitably you will get terrible chemicals. As a result of my quest to chase an impossible feeling of satisfaction and Austin's impossible lust for my money, I would spend every moment of my time thinking of new ways to carry on with this degrading lifestyle. Almost every waking moment I wished I could find a way to end the madness, with the rules of the world suddenly changing at my bequest. To quote a million and one cockneys, 'I didn't have a clue'.

Despite the repetitive, depressing underworld I inhabited, the next six months of my life would prove to be beyond normal comprehension.

★ ★ ★

On a late Wednesday evening, flushed with cash, Austin and I made our way to the supplier of the purest crystal white cocaine within a ten mile radius. We made sure we had the usual cab driver, who was asked to give us a lift in exchange for money 'next week and a tenner on top'. I pulled on my headphones while we drove in the dusty old people carrier to the darkest depths of South London. I was aware that the dealer would expect to be bartered with, so I was already planning my rebuttals and reasons for getting the best bits and the extra bits.

Despite his well-built frame, Jekke was only five feet eight inches. His braided hair was always well-oiled and perfectly groomed, even on a weekday. His presence was always disconcerting and dominant. He made no unnecessary attempts at conversation, often contrasting with the person he was dealing with. He moved with the shadowy actions of a man who could blend into the streets. Stepping into his hallway, one could pick up the faint smell of designer cologne. It gave the impression that he was always ready to head out into the night for business or pleasure. His clothes were often yellow and black, with pristine jackets and caps, while the Timberland boots he wore showed no evidence of ever having been worn outside.

He had an effective way of communicating, utilising his heritage. If he wanted something specific or was happy with the dealings going on, he would use an easy to understand London accent with a slow, measured pace. If he was displeased or deliberately wary, he would use a native Jamaican accent with an incredibly fast tempo, which I found almost impossible to understand.

'What do you want?' he asked.

'An eight ball and all the good stuff,' I said with authority.

He unravelled a brown envelope, the kind that would usually hold someone's cash wages. The rustling inside produced six pieces of rock wrapped in several layers of film. These were handed over to me in exchange for a collection of notes.

As we travelled back in our cab, I held onto half the substance in my mouth. The taste of plastic made me want to choke and I concentrated on the nausea rising in my stomach, trying to remind myself that it would pass as soon as we were inside and the poison hit my throat. I was very aware that we were expecting visitors and this produce would be shared with other hungry mouths, none of whom were invited by me. When we reached the flat, I was told that we would be meeting a couple called Patrick and Amanda.

Both of them were in their early thirties, like me. Patrick was six feet tall with untidy, shoulder-length hair. Amanda had long black hair tied back, but you could tell it would fall down the middle of her back if let loose. They were inseparable and co-dependent. They were relatively well-off and spoke with well-educated London accents, yet the decay of the drug world was already seeping into their eyes and skin tone. Patrick was dressed in a long overcoat and dark but trendy clothes, whilst Amanda wore tight jeans and a designer wooly jumper. Patrick looked long overdue for a shave.

'It's nice of you to share this with us,' said Amanda. I nodded with approval and smiled halfheartedly. 'You know, if you had some spare cash we know where to get some pukker gear.'

'Shall we use this first?' I said with disdain.

'Yeah, but you know we're only saying it to help you out, yeah?' she bounced back in a mixture of what I can only describe as Jamaican and cockney. 'Ja-faking.'

I smoked a hit and tried to think of a way to end this conversation. I knew they were users and my anxiety level was now rising rapidly, which promoted the idea that these people were already ruining my night. My mind tussled over the idea that this was the type of person I was destined to become.

'So I can go and get it now, yeah?' said Patrick. 'And then there's no gap.'

'Listen, I don't want to spend any more money,' I replied.

'Oh, I see,' said Amanda, raising her voice whilst the cocaine gave her unnatural energy.

'What do you see?' I quickly retorted.

'So, we come all the way over here to keep you company and you treat us like this.'

'I'm not treating you like anything. I've bought this stuff and spent my money and invited you over to enjoy it.'

'Oh, so now it's all about your money and how we are so lucky.'

'No, that doesn't make sense,' I said. 'What's your problem? You should be grateful to me.'

Both Patrick and Amanda jumped up and moved into a space that made their presence felt. You could see the desperate anger in their eyes, masking the reality and reasoning for their behaviour. Patrick turned his back on the room and moved over to the kitchen.

'You can go fuck yourself, yeah,' he spat.

I laughed nervously and looked to Austin for some support. Before I could think of anything useful to do or say, I saw Patrick holding a large carving knife with a crazed look in his eye. Amanda saw her boyfriend's strategy and began to smirk.

'Well now, you smug prick,' she said nastily. 'We're going to take all the stuff you bought with your precious money.'

They scrambled for the rocks on the table, whilst smiling and wheezing in delight. My eye was still firmly cast on the knife and I could feel my heart beating through my chest. I made a decision at that moment that I needed to change my life and quickly. These people were warped and, although I was by no means perfect, I always knew where to draw the line and how to maintain the fragment of my soul that stopped me turning into the people I secretly despised.

★ ★ ★

The next day, I sat in the park in the freezing cold and watched apparently normal people pass between different exit points at the gates. Although I have come to realise that people from all walks of life carry many different secrets and moods, it was the vision of the normal working life that I once knew that haunted me. I was meeting my friend Ben. We had arranged to meet here as it was of equal distance from both our starting points; I found it incredibly important to make sure that journeys were as short as possible for both parties, as long as adequate seating was available.

Ben was tall, about six foot two. His hair was short, blond and, as far as I was concerned, completely ridiculous. Despite being short almost all over, the front portion was longer and, over the last few months, I had noticed this piece being gelled across his forehead. I saw this as an attempt to avert the descent into a receding hairline as, from the middle of the head backwards, the hair was spiky. I remembered a time I once saw inside his wardrobe while he preened himself before going out; there were multiple bottles of hair gel lined up on the top shelf, like a collection of fine wines. I predicted at the time that this collection would be obsolete for him within a year. This was not taken well, evidenced by the look of utter misery that painted his face for the following week.

Ben moved over to the bench with a great slowness that irritated me enormously. I, however, welcomed the irritation because I loved winding him up about almost anything, his reaction always childlike and ridiculous. Whatever this said about me was certainly not good, but I just couldn't help it.

'Look, I've got a new bet on,' Ben proclaimed.

'Well, I'm sure you have a winner.'

'I have mate, seriously.'

'If it's another accumulator made up of sixty odd matches with a lonely pound coin as the stake, then I'm sure you'll do just fine.'

'Well, it's nine matches and I have a fiver on it. If I win, the pot's one hundred and eighty pounds payout,' Ben drawled out in his Manchester accent.

He laughed with the excited glee of a kid at Disneyland and pulled out a cigarette almost as if he was programmed to do so every time. He had smothered himself in Lynx deodorant as if it really did attract all women to the scent, like the adverts suggested. I sometimes wondered if all humans would be like him in a hundred years. It was a shame that, in my opinion, he actually smelt of propellant and something similar to wood polish.

'I'm heading to Thailand, mate, to go to a treatment centre. It's supposed to be the toughest regime in the world,' I said quickly.

'But why you going out there to do that? You'll be alright over here. I can help you!'

'No mate. Over there it's a prison that locks you in for a minimum of two weeks. No drugs, no comfort and no escape.'

'Why the fuck would you want to do that?'

'Because I can't do this same old thing anymore with the same old people,' I said with venom. 'Everyone is getting crazier and the scene is seedier and I'm sick of it.'

★ ★ ★

I could hardly feel the plane take off, lulled to sleep in comforting insanity and slowly dispersing alcohol. I started to dream of my destination and what could be, but the faint horror of reality was always ticking in my ear.

Woken up for the first time during the flight, a stewardess offered me my food. I took the tray but I knew instantly that I would not eat and, therefore, I did not look. The size of my stomach was very small, from a combination of pills, syrups and adult beverages. These not only disintegrated my digestion, but they held my instincts at bay and freed up my time to consume more narcotics and create deluded plans of grandeur.

I took the opportunity to order another drink. I asked for a quadruple Vodka on ice. My mind had a locked-in process for ordering spirits without mixers, just in case the juice interfered with the drink penetrating my stomach lining. Obviously, I knew this was nonsense and, if anything, the alcohol would dilute and travel more easily into the bloodstream, but my brain still told me that the purer the substance the more likely I was to feel it. I remembered back to the days when I would queue for hours to get into nightclub toilets with an alphabet soup of toxins.

In the last ten years, the mainstream nightclubs that were previously all about the drinking and the flirting had become completely focused on subversive dance tracks and industrial-strength party drugs. People say that drugs have become more diluted and less people are taking them, but the myth is more complicated than people would have you imagine. If you know the right people, then you can get anything and, even if you don't, there are more substitute chemicals now than there are illegal substances. As cocaine becomes diluted or terribly expensive, crystal meth moves in to take its place. Where ecstasy has become heavily mixed and hard to find, mephedrone has taken its place on the dance floor.

★ ★ ★

I was barely awake for much of the flight. The captain

actually had to wake me up, as the polite manner of the stewardesses had failed to nudge me out of my slumber.

When I had managed to pick up my bags from arrivals and slowly shuffled out towards the taxi area of Bangkok airport, I sat my bags down and used the railings as a prop to create a makeshift seat. As soon as I rested in any position or on any type of object, I would fall back to sleep. I saw a young man about the same age as me nudge his sunglasses and focus his gaze. He followed this up by making his way over to me.

Jarvis was of medium height and small in build, and in his late twenties. He had messy dark hair and wore Ray Ban sunglasses. I instantly assumed he was American. He moved with a nervousness and slightness that suggested he was also far away from home. He was wearing expensive summer clothes that showed quality and style. His LA voice was used sparingly and was surprisingly deep for the overall appearance he presented. Despite the stereotypical image of Americans being suntanned and with pearly white smiles, this guy has pale skin and sunken eyes to match the cigarette-stained teeth. It was obvious to me at this point that he was the other Westerner who was meant to be sharing a cab ride to the rehab. Somehow, over the years, I had developed an ability to recognise drug takers and drug users very easily. In my hazed mind filled with Benzos, painkillers and alcohol, this was my only certainty.

'Hey man, so you're sharing the taxi to the joint?' he said.

'Yeah. Let me know when it arrives,' I said rudely.

With that, I fell asleep again, only to be woken by the

taxi driver who wanted to load the bags into the car. Without helping a single bit with this process, I lit up a cigarette and drank the final dregs of some methadone I had. My only regret at that point was that I hadn't bought more. The next few hours' drive to the 'joint' was extremely short in my head and I spoke not one word to Jarvis, except to ask if he knew how the seats reclined. I imagine he was thinking I was an arsehole, but the beautiful thing about heavy narcotics is the completely impenetrable wall they create in your mind to avoid any thought of criticism or true concept of reality.

★ ★ ★

We eventually arrive in the three-mile square location for the prison-style rehab. It is impossible to describe it as anything other than beautiful. The sun was beaming down and humid air strikes the senses instantly. The greenery was everywhere, enhancing the ethereal sky overhead. Little shops and houses were littered around, while the car was the loudest thing to pass through the area. The only people we could see on our way in were Buddhist monks. They were dressed in brown robes with a sash that covered their torso. Their eyes penetrated into the car as we arrived, but my consciousness was minimal and the only thought I could muster was that I needed a bed. The air seemed fresh and clean, but it felt unfamiliar and created a sense of anxiety. However, I pushed it away in my mind with the existing toxins in my brain.

A young monk took my belongings and passed them over to a nun. She rigorously unzipped my bags and started going through them with the energy of a US customs official.

'Am I allowed to take my belongings into the camp'? I asked in a dry, raspy voice.

'No, you will only be allowed some basic toiletries,' was the nun's response.

'What about my clothes?' I asked in a slightly more concerned voice.

'Didn't you read the contract? You will be given shorts and shirt, but no outside clothes allowed.'

'What contract? The entry form?' I enquired with a puzzled tone.

The nun simply ignored my last statement and told a younger monk to take me into a small cubicle. As the monk led me along by the arm, I again felt an impending doom which I still couldn't put my finger on. He instructed me in broken English to remove my clothes and put them into a bag; however, when I started to remove my jeans, I remembered that I had put around a dozen painkillers in my boxer shorts. I tried to get undressed in the manner of an elderly gentleman protecting frail bones and delicate muscles; however, this only served to arouse the suspicion of the young monk, who was eyeballing me with crossed arms.

As the impending incarceration had become to feel much more serious, I was determined to keep the painkillers come hell or high water. I thought I was succeeding in my task, despite looking either really stoned or stupid, until we both heard a small tap on the floor. I looked at the monk with a puzzled look and continued to reach over to the prison issue shorts. As I lifted my leg into the first side of the shorts, we both heard another tap and, without missing a beat, the young monk put a hand on my boxer shorts and pulled back the lining to reveal the dull, white pills that surrounded my crotch.

'What is this?' he asked quietly.

'I don't know,' I replied unconvincingly. 'I must have put them there for some reason.'

Very quickly I began to pull out the pills and handed them to the monk. He went outside the cubicle and I could only assume he chucked the pills away and alerted the others to my failed attempt at smuggling. I was not off to the best of starts and I began to feel that the situation was going to become a whole lot worse.

The camp comprised three small buildings. One contained the squatting toilets, one was for the Thai prisoners, while the other was for the Western volunteer patients. There were numerous statues of worship inside the camp and Thai national flags. Upon entering the Western camp, I immediately saw the very humble conditions we would be staying in. The door, which was hanging off its hinges, was made out of old mesh wire. There were two old ceiling fans, one of which was broken and covered in small lizards.

As I head inside the room I can hear the Thai prisoners speaking in high-pitched voices from across the way, while even further in the distance I can hear the sound of machinery working on the statues that line the compound. I kick away a mattress, the kind you would get in gym class at school. I can smell the stench of BO and stale cigarettes emanating from the plastic surface. The temperature is so hot that the smells from the camp seemed to ride over my tiredness, and the new bed that was now laid out before me was becoming increasingly unappealing.

★ ★ ★

As night time approached I could feel the cold sweats beginning to take over my body and it was impossible to sit comfortably. Jarvis was next to me in the room and, despite admitting to a terrible habit, he was sleeping fairly quickly. I knew that I would not be getting any sleep, but I hoped that the physical sensations wouldn't get any worse and that, with time, I would get better.

The night dragged on forever. I tossed and turned on the plastic mattress with nothing to hold onto for comfort, and it was at this point that the effects of sleep deprivation added to my misery. What made relaxation even more difficult was the incessant howling of the husky-type dogs that roamed the grounds. There were six dogs that protected the camp and their nocturnal activities included fighting, barking and hunting. I would watch the Geckos run around the ceiling as if unaware of the laws of gravity and I kept myself on a constant state of alert in case one decided to join me on the mattress, while throughout the nightmare of the night the dogs would growl and prowl amidst the inescapable camp. When I got up in the morning, the nausea and aches I experienced caused me to consider whether I should try and drown myself in a cup of tea, but I then remembered that a normal English cup of tea would not be available.

I went through the paces of the programme and didn't manage to utter a word to my detoxing colleagues until the steam bath portion that day. The steam bath was a two-hut shack set up on the outer grounds, near what appeared to be some type of wood-cutting site. Next to the baths was a large wooden tub which, in some ways, looked just like a medieval jacuzzi. It turned out to be a trough for collecting bowls of cold water and dousing oneself after a steam. Next to the baths was a hot water dispenser, where we were then instructed to drink quickly before entering the steam. I couldn't understand the reason for this and why we couldn't just drink cold water and be done with it.

'What's in this tea, may I ask?' I said to the nearest monk, who was watching the line of inductees with stern disapproval.

'Niacin.'

I chose not to enquire any further about the tea and drank some quickly. What I would later discover was that Niacin, in large quantities, acts by clearing toxins stored in the body fat and organs. Some experts have suggested that it can bring on drug re-stimulations as it reheats and leaves the body. Inside the baths, I found myself squashed in with about ten other people. As I sat next to Jarvis, I noticed that he was looking decidedly pale and ill; however, despite the fact I was feeling like death warmed up, I decided to enquire into his current state, simply so that I wouldn't feel so alone.

'Awful and sick,' he hissed. 'This whole thing is killing me.'

'Me too. I don't honestly know how I'm going to make it through.'

With that short exchange I knew that Jarvis was going to be my only hope of any friendship in this place. It made me feel bad that I had treated him with what appeared to be disdain on the way in, but at the same time I also knew from his obvious physical decline that no explanation was necessary.

I had been dreading the vomit portion of the day and, when the time arrived, I decided to take the fatalistic approach: that the way I was feeling couldn't get any worse and, therefore, the vomiting might actually help me in some way. The courtyard where the vomiting took place was the size of a five-a-side football pitch. A drainage system ran along the sides, and marble tiling paved the line in order that the vomitees could see where they should line up.

A group of long-term dwellers, who no longer had to puke, gathered in a group and held religious signs whilst chanting a mantra. Around the pitch there were at least twenty people who began to sit cross-legged on the ground, while the monks began to hand out bowls and buckets full of water. The whole time the chanting mantra and tambourine sounds were ringing in my ears and the overall sense of occasion momentarily distracted me from my pain. I glanced at Jarvis and saw that he was looking just as fragile. We both looked to the left to see an older monk carrying a bottle of black liquid and shot glasses. Despite the knowledge that this was going to be a hard time, I tried to pretend that this was just some sick drinking game in an effort to prevent my mind from combusting into a million stressed-out pieces. I passed this information on to Jarvis, who simply showed a brief forced smirk before sinking back into his misery.

The monk approached me and poured the liquid into a shot glass, which I then drunk without hesitation. He gestured me to take the dog bowl and start swallowing water as quickly as possible. As I started to force the slightly dirty-looking water into my mouth, I felt the twinge of nausea hit me like an assassin's bullet. The vile taste seemed to hit me from all angles and started a war with my insides. It seemed imperative to get this stuff out. I noticed that Jarvis was beginning to heave and so, with a sharp finger to the throat, I pushed half a litre of brown water out of my body. On an almost rhythmic setting, Jarvis and I took turns to vomit the salty, dirt-laden liquid out until I could feel my eyes popping out of their sockets.

'I really don't feel normal, Jarvis,' I said quietly.

'I haven't felt normal in years,' was all he had to say.

After another sleepless night I was ready to do it all over again. During opiate withdrawal, the first three days are the worst with diarrhoea, vomiting and a general sense of agony. It's probably worth mentioning that the depression you feel can last for anything up to two weeks after stopping the drugs, and you will start a habit again just too dull the senses.

As I stumbled around on day three I could feel my kidneys aching, while my legs felt like they had tiny hot knives coursing through their veins. As a consequence, my head was hurting worse than ever, and the fact that the only place I could wash would take first prize as the worst bathroom in the world, complete with blocked piss-soaked toilets and a hose attached to the wall to wash, I was feeling pretty shabby. The problem with this bathroom was more to do with the fact that, when you sat down on it, your balls would drop in the dirty water and the flies would buzz around your head when you tried to relieve yourself. Now, the one thing I require in this world as a 'must have' is a clean, working bathroom; that is why, since the age of seventeen, I refused to go to any music festival. This, however, was worse than any porter potty – especially after the new guy, 'Alexei, The Mad Russian', arrived.

Alexei was as tall as me and built like Jabba the Hut. Jabba the Hut, for anyone who doesn't know, was a character from *Star Wars* who, in essence, was a massive disgusting monster. His personality was not at all like the image, but his profile fitted everything you would imagine in an ex-police officer come gangster from eastern Europe. He moved only between his bed and the plastic chairs outside our dorm in order to continue chain smoking. Like me, he sat up all night with insomnia. He was always sweaty and dressed in his red uniform like the rest of us, so he looked harmless. The question as to whether he was or not remained unanswered, as it was a strange place to get to know someone. He spoke in broken English, which was his only way of communicating with the monks or with his fellow inmates and, given that he was a hardened alcoholic and withdrawing hard, I felt sorry for him. The only time I didn't feel sorry for him was when he went to the bathroom to drop the mother load and then carried on as normal as I entered to find what could only be described as utter carnage.

As Jarvis was American, I could only assume that his natural dislike for Alexei was based on some slightly old-fashioned propaganda ideology.

'That fat sweaty fuck Russian is really pissing me off. I don't even feel safe to fall asleep with him around,' he said with force.

'You can't sleep anyway. Well, you get some sleep, but not exactly a lot,' I replied.

'I really want to do my minimum ten days and get out of here. Go relax,' he retorts.

'What do you mean, a minimum of ten days?'

'You have to stay ten days as agreed on the contract. If you try to leave, they keep all your stuff and even your passport and they call the cops.'

'Fuck that!'

With this news, I began to panic. Even though I was halfway through, the pressure of knowing I had no say and couldn't bail if I wanted made me very angry. The minutes and hours that followed ticked by like slow motion and the sickness began to win the fight again.

That night, I didn't even bother to try and sleep; instead, I sat outside with Alexei and tried to make sympathetic faces at him while he spoke the same ten to fifteen English words he knew. Despite the obvious shortcomings in the conversation, Alexei managed to tell me quite a few facts of his life. I was intrigued to know why he was now living in Thailand and how he supported himself.

As we slowly made our way through the conversation, I could feel my legs aching and kicking, which was an effect of the opiate withdrawal. One of the main reasons people can't sleep or rest when they come off heroin is because of the pain in their legs. To me, it felt like the nerve endings in my legs were loose electrical wires flailing about desperately in protest. Sometimes, when I was sure nobody could see, I would tie a rolled-up t-shirt around each one of my calves and inflict some necessary pain and disrupt the blood flow like a tourniquet.

Anyway, back to Alexei. He was born in Moscow, Russia, fifty years ago. He was born into a tough family with political connections and he had three older brothers. In 1992, when the country dropped communism, Alexei became a policeman and, like many police working in the city of Moscow, there were fringe benefits, but most felt that these were fair as the salary was the equivalent of two hundred Euros a month. On-the-spot driving penalties were the most consistent cash-earners, with tourists becoming easy prey. Thailand had a similar method, so what he saw out on the streets over here was just a home away from home. As his gut size increased and his ego grew, acquiring money became a more creative exercise, from pirate films being sold on street corners in their hundreds to the seizure and redistribution of weapons. Over time he built up a considerable nest egg.

Family and close friends appeared to be on his mind frequently and he worried about the friend who had brought him in, when he had been in a terrible drunken state. On the other side of the coin, Alexei would finish any discussion on the friend who brought him in to our camp by saying that he would kill him as soon as he was able.

'If you get out and you want to stay for a while?' he said in long, drawn-out words.

'I can come see you, can I?'

'Yes. I have very nice apartment and many new cars. I have power there... but I have to escape from this stupid place first.' He gestured with a sweeping hand to the camp.

I noticed he wasn't wearing any footwear, which was an unusual and dangerous thing to do in the camp considering the amount of insects that infested the place.

'Where are your sandals?' I gestured towards his feet.

'I do not know. I can only find one. Not where I left it.'

'So you have no shoes. That can't be a good thing.'

'I think the dog has taken it. The small dog that play here.'

I tried to think of the dog he meant and assumed it was Laika, the husky puppy that liked to stray from the pact and play with the Westerners. Laika was a blonde and white husky that appeared to be the youngest of the pact. Unlike the other dogs, she was quiet and friendly and sometimes mischievous. She would constantly beg you to play at any opportunity and would eat anything you gave her. As a young pup, she was similar in mentality to the dogs I was used to in Britain and had none of the aggressive qualities that the other dogs shared in the camp. She was fast and agile, constantly playing with any object or person that crossed her path. It was almost as if she didn't get along with the other dogs and preferred human interaction. Sometimes you would see her join in the pact and get quickly ousted by her brothers and sisters.

The next day, I saw Alexei walk up to one of the senior monks and, from what I could make out, he was explaining about his sandals going missing. He showed the one remaining sandal to the monk and I could see that something was about to be done. Within an hour the monk had found a collection of sandals rounded up at the back of our building, a place where Laika liked to hide out. The image of the monk carrying half a dozen mixed sandals was very amusing, given that the dog appeared to have some kind of shoe fetish. I put this action down to attention-seeking and I couldn't help but feel a great affection for the dog and the distraction from the daily grind was most welcome.

Unfortunately, the outcome for Laika was quite horrendous. Shortly after the steam baths that day, I noticed Laika was hobbling around the camp and unusually she would not come over to our section to play. I headed over to the pitch area where the dogs were mostly sleeping and eating and called her over. As she hobbled over to me I noticed that her back legs had been tied together with string and she couldn't do anything about it. I felt furious and upset. Standing up, I marched over to the monks who were sitting drinking tea by the gate. I walked straight up to the most senior monk and he caught my eye instantly.

'Why is the dog tied?' I said, making a rope impression with my hands.

'She takes the shoes,' he said solemnly.

'But she is just a dog, she doesn't understand.'

'She needs to learn. Very important.'

'Like I said, she doesn't understand.'

'In Thailand we know how to train our dogs. Very different here.'

With that last comment, a younger monk grabbed a home-made sling shot and picked up a rock. I watched with horror as he pulled back the band, aimed and fired at Laika, hitting her in the abdomen and causing her to cry out. With all the pain I felt from my own physical and mental withdrawal, I was not strong enough to change anything here and, despite the deep sadness and anger I felt at what these people were doing, I couldn't do anything about it. Instead, I went and sat in a corner and beckoned Laika over to me, where I then sat and petted her for close to two hours. I genuinely felt helpless at that point, more so than I had in a long time.

During the last two days of mandatory confinement, I gradually began to feel hope and excitement again. The pain had almost gone from my body by day eight and, although I hadn't slept at all during my stay, the sun during the day gave me the natural energy to get through. Despite the agony I had gone through, I knew that I was going to leave on day ten. I wanted nothing more than to go to a hotel, drink some alcohol, eat some good food and sleep in a nice crisp comfortable bed. I was exhausted and the very idea I had painted in my head seemed like Nirvana. I had often discussed this idea with Jarvis and he, too, having felt the weight of the long week hitting him like a brick to the head, felt that he would come with me.

On day nine, Jarvis and I went with a nun to the internet and phone hut, which was located in the grounds about half a mile away. Unfortunately for Jarvis, the plan of escape from the camp was going to become impossible. Upon reading his e-mails, he discovered that impending charges for possession of drugs back in LA were dependent on him being in a rehab and proving, beyond a shadow of a doubt, that he had been clean and healthy for three months. Not only this, but the rehab we were in was being researched by the prosecution as to whether it could be valid for use in his case.

I could see that the news was heart-breaking for him and that the idea of either going to jail or staying in the camp was almost too much to bear. I also had to come to terms with the fact that, if I wanted to get some much-needed sleep and get out, I was going to have to do this alone. Being in a country like Thailand, and having just recovered from a massive withdrawal from numerous drugs, this was a risky and frightening prospect. My lust for rest and normality, however, kept the thirst alive. I approached the monks that night and arranged for a local taxi driver to pick me up the next day.

★ ★ ★

In Elmira, New York, on Tuesday 26 January 1892, between 2 and 3 am, Dr Adele Gleason dreamt she stood in a lonesome place in the dark woods and that great fear came over her, at which point she dreamt that John Joslyn, her attorney and friend, came to her and shook a tree by her, causing its leaves to burst into flame. When the two friends met four days later, Adele mentioned having had a 'strange dream' the previous Tuesday night. John stopped her at once.

'Don't tell it to me,' he said. 'Let me describe it, for I know that I dreamt the same thing.'

At approximately the same time as Adele's strange dream, John had awoken from a no less strange dream of his own and written down the following, remarkably similar, account.

He had found Adele in a lonely wood after dark, 'apparently paralysed with fear by something I did not see, rooted to the spot by the feeling of imminent danger. I came up to her and shook the bush, upon which the leaves that fell from it burst into flame.'

★ ★ ★

Ginoh was described to me on two fronts before I left in the taxi. Alexei, who lived there, told me that it had a beach, lots of bars and Westerners, and beautiful women. He did, however, explain that there were lots of women who looked like women but actually were something entirely different. The process by which he explained the checklist he used to differentiate was quite disgusting, but almost entirely essential.

The taxi took hours to get me to my destination. I had been promised a fare of no more than two thousand Baht, but I could see the meter already hitting two and a half. The heat that hit me inside the taxi was immense and, despite air-conditioning, the LPG-powered Nissan was like an electric oven. I asked to switch on the radio and hear some music, given that conversation was virtually impossible. What came out the speakers was a variety of classic rock from the eighties and Thai rock music, which consisted of sultry love songs in high-pitched voices and solo guitar.

'Where would you like to stay?' the taxi driver asked.

'In a nice hotel. I would also like a pharmacy.'

'I don't understand.'

'Medicine, painkillers.'

'Ah, medicine! And hotel. How much?'

'Small money,' I said, keeping to the smallest sentence possible. It seemed to be the best way for me to communicate.

There were thousands of people as we entered Ginoh. Before I had left the camp, an English nun had told me that the town was like 'the Wild West'. She told me I shouldn't go and I wouldn't enjoy it. I decided that anything being described as the Wild West could only be a good thing. My mind had become increasingly robust in thinking this way, always looking for the meaning between the lines and not the meaning that was being spelt out for me. Thousands of people crawled through the streets like ants and the cars were wedged into any space possible. Horns and sirens and music crossed through my ears like arrows and I started to feel a hint of anxiety. I did, however, keep reminding myself that soon I would rest and then, maybe, I could play. The anxiety then turned into full-blown adrenaline.

We arrived at what I could only describe as a boutique hotel situated on the hills, just above the beach resort area. It was quiet compared to the main drive in, but still I could see a mesh of bars, pharmacies and street carts full of delicious-looking treats. The smell of pork and rich sauces wafted through the air and I began to feel relaxed. I was dressed in my own clothes, a selection of designer shirt and jeans with five hundred pound cowboy boots I had bought in London. For the first time in a long time I was free from addiction and motoring along like any normal person, which made me feel quite ecstatic. Despite the dreadful sleep deprivation and a feeling that I could do with a proper wash, I knew that I was back in the game. I tipped the taxi driver and went to my room, having checked in and paid for my one night.

When I entered the room I could almost feel my brain tingle with excitement at the sight of the modern, clean bathroom. I kept repeating the mantra 'simple things', over and over as I walked around the air-conditioned room. The sheets on the bed felt cold and soft, while the next thing I saw made me smile from ear to ear. A flat screen TV was perched on the wall and I greeted it with open arms as if worshiping a lost antiquity.

Once I had gotten over the initial euphoria, I made a solemn promise that I would not enjoy any of these luxuries until I had frequented the chemist. The programming in my brain to relate happiness with chemicals was unnerving even to me, and the subsequent thought was that I wanted Valium, simple Valium. Nature's foot soldier in the aid of sleep and goodwill. The assassin of anxiety and negativity. The bearer of deep, relaxing slumber. I did not want painkillers or stimulants, or any other such thing; I simply wanted to medicate myself like a sensible, modern, twenty-first century guy with the goal of becoming even stronger and healthier and well-rested. The mental gymnastics I did to fool myself into believing these things began to jar me, so before I could think too deeply I went off, money in hand, to fulfil my mission.

The chemists were littered everywhere and had the appearance of fine wine shops, with better detailing and paintwork than any other shop around. As I walked into one of the air-conditioned shops, I immediately saw a packet stand on the counter offering alprazolam (Xanax) in bundles of twelve. Next to the Xanax was another offer for Tramadol – an opiate analgesic synthetic usually used after tooth surgery. With the offer laid out in front of me, I decided to buy a packet of each. I justified buying the Tramadol because I knew that it was not a true opiate and had a low addiction level; therefore, as the strong man I believe I had become, I could handle these and I would soon feel the relief sent from God that I imagined these tablets would deliver.

Back safely in my room, I took some of the tablets and undressed myself for what I believed would be a long, wonderful sleep. I switched the TV on, just to flip through the channels whist the pills kicked in. My sense of distrust told me that these pills might not work, or that I may have been ripped off and poisoned. I lit up a cigarette and lay hovering in euphoria on the crisp sheets, a feeling that was without parallel after the ten days in camp. The TV had a channel which showed only English speaking films, obviously designed for the tourist and, for me at this point, an amazingly exciting innovation.

Soon I drifted off and woke up, many hours later, with the sun-drenched windows now dark and unnerving. The sleep, which was obviously needed, had left me with a strong sense of disassociation and a mild hangover feeling, the kind you get from eating too much carbohydrate before you sleep. A cigarette and a beer from the minibar was the combination I utilised to wake me up. I needed to get my shit together and chase that euphoria I felt when I arrived. The highs and lows of my mind had become more and more disparate over the last few years and I didn't want to spend any time analysing them.

I headed off into the centre of town, following the sound of loud music and the bustle of drunken strangers. In the near distance I could see that the crowds were descending into what looked like a giant modern version of the yellow brick road. A sign that announced 'Standing Street' lined the width of the entrance some twenty feet above their heads I could hear the sounds of claxons, whooping and hollering, and the crackle of tasers being demonstrated from street vendors.

As I walked through into the buzzing street, I found myself distracted by the many stalls that sold a variant of weapons. They had everything from guns, samurai swords, flick knives and electrical weapons. I stopped at a stall where a man was trying out a butterfly knife. The smell of gunpowder and alcohol was overpowering as I stood watching the illicit weapons in the still boiling temperature and humidity. My t-shirt was sticking to my back with sweat and the constant stream of cigarette smoke was filtering into the material.

'Do you sell body armour?' I asked, tapping my front.

'Body armour?' the vendor said.

'Bulletproof vest?'

'Ah, something to stop gun.'

'Yes. Or a knife,' I said warily, as I watched other customers giving me glances.

'Yes. I have special outside back. I cannot sell out here on street.'

'Ok. I'll come back, my friend.'

I had been told by a friend back home, who was the owner of a security firm, that out in Thailand, or most parts of Asia, you could buy these vests for a fraction of the price. At home they could cost as much as a thousand pounds or more. Over here, the price would be more like fifty pounds. I was always interested in a good deal, and if it was something useful and exciting I found it hard not to buy it. Given some of the dangerous situations I had been in over the last ten years, something like an armour vest was very appealing, and part of my psyche liked the idea of giving people a symbolic message wrapped around my torso. 'Back off!'

I sauntered through the streets of this tourist hot spot and stopped every so often to look through windows of tattoo parlours and strip bars. The place made Soho look like a day care centre, while every hundred yards there would be brothels with women pouring out of the upper balconies and screaming dirty innuendo at the men outside. Eventually I came across a small bar with contemporary dance music blaring out from behind a red curtain. I recognised the music as extremely up-to-date club music, the kind I would hear back home. Given that I was surrounded by foreign exposure and beginning to feel slightly lonely, I decided that maybe the nostalgic beats of the music would cheer me up. It also struck me that there would probably be something exciting to find in there.

As I approached the red curtain, I was ushered over to a man standing by an old-fashioned till. He asked for five hundred Baht, which I paid. The curtain was parted and I could see a small bar to the left with two, quite ugly-looking girls sulking into their hands. The music was indeed loud and, in the very back of the room, higher up than anywhere else, a chubby Thai man was mixing records. The floor was sticky and the smell of aniseed hit my nose. There were only a few people around but they mostly seemed like workers, while the few Westerners in the bar were drinking by themselves.

I headed over to the barmaid and asked for a Long Island Iced Tea. This drink had been my favourite for years, as it had as much alcohol as you could get in a glass; it tasted good and it stayed down easily. I swallowed the drink and sat at the bar, thinking about my next move. As I did so, I noticed a small, young-looking man sitting next to me.

'What are you looking for?' he asked.

'Few drinks, good time,' I said.

'I can take you to the best places. I own this place.'

He appeared a little slimy and insincere, but I wasn't completely sure of what to make of him because I was in such as strange country.

'You like sexy women? I can get the best,' he slithered.

'Ok. Well, you know, I'll see how it goes,' I said nonchalantly.

Once again, he appeared to give off a bad radar signal to me. He went off back towards the red curtain and, from his interactions with the other men around him, I assumed he was the leader of sorts. His sharp, cutting movements and mannerism made him look somewhat aggressive. As I sat finishing my first Long Island, I ordered a follow-up drink of two shots of tequila and vodka Red Bull. The mixture of the first strong drink permeating into my stomach wall and hitting the bloodstream with full velocity had put me into a secondary drinking state, in which I would order the stronger sets of rounds even if I was the only one there. Force of habit.

'I have got you this. Yes. The very best from Thailand,' a familiar voice said suddenly.

I look around and saw the little boss of the bar sitting next to me holding two red pills in the palm of his hand. I looked at them and, despite my encyclopaedic knowledge of drugs in general, couldn't recognise them. It was at this point, as I became heavily over the drink drive limit, that even the horrendously ugly barmaid became less horrendous and, as a consequence, everything was distracting. Two little pills were not going to be of interest.

'This is Yabba,' the snake said.

I had heard of Yabba but never seen it. It is considered to be so dangerous that, in England, the border guards are on the lookout for derivatives of it as much as they look for heroin and cocaine. It has not managed to make it over to the UK, but that hasn't stopped journalists talking about it every so often. A picture struck my mind of a scene in Bangkok, several years before, where a man who was binging on Yabba ended up having a full psychosis outside the airport and held his daughter like a human sacrifice, with a huge hunting knife in his hands. The thing that struck me about the picture was that the man's eyes had rolled back in his head and all you could see was the white of his eyeballs. The image was terrifying.

'Yabba. I've never had it,' I said as I contemplated the positives and negatives.

'You feel good, you know. Warm rush and lots of energy.'

'How much?'

'You give me two thousand Baht,' he said, which sounded an awful lot of money for where we were.

Against my own good judgement, I pulled out the money and gave it to him, but before he handed over the pills he went back over to the curtain and spoke to his colleagues. When he sauntered back over, he handed me one of them and swallowed the other.

'We go somewhere good,' he said.

'You and me?' I asked nervously.

'Yes. Follow me and we go and see very beautiful girls.'

A few minutes later, we were walking briskly over to a better decorated part of town. As I walked along, I noticed that the men started to look older and were smartly dressed, with the appearance of the Costa Del Crime retirees that you would see in other parts of the world. We arrived at the bar and were ushered into a very Western-looking lap dancing club. The employees and higher ranking management greeted us with adoring faces and sycophantic behaviour. It was odd to see this young, skinny-looking man being treated with such austerity.

Within a minute, I could see a tray of drinks being brought over, despite the fact I hadn't ordered anything, and laid out before me were several shots of Sambuca with the complimentary coffee beans floating in the top of the glass. It was around this point that I could feel a surge of adrenaline floating into my veins from the pill. I was dubious as to whether the pills were duds, but now that the little red drops had started to infiltrate into me I could feel my excitement increasing and my inhibitions disappearing.

After I paid for the first few rounds by leaving cash on conveniently placed trays, the young host leant in to tell me of the next plan.

'Ok. You have more money and we see the very best girls now.'

'Well, actually I'm all out.'

The look on his face turned to stone. His eyes were the kind of dark brown lifeless eyes that I had seen in countless sociopaths over the years. I couldn't see his pupils and the almost inhuman minimal movements sent off all the wrong signals.

'Well, we go back to your hotel and you get money.'

The humour and friendliness gone, his eyes dictated that this was an order and not a request. I could feel the impending danger immediately and, like so many pseudo criminal gangs that I had encountered, the others within this venue knew that he was displeased. It also struck me that I had a dangerous narcotic in me spinning countless threads of adrenaline. Unlike a lot of people, I operate best sober and can be much more controlling and aggressive in dangerous situations when I'm drug-free. In this state, I felt that I was in no position to argue.

'Ok. We'll go back,' I said reluctantly.

We took a taxi bike back to the hotel. The tiny moped felt very uneasy and, what with three people dangling over rough ground and with the impending danger I could sense, I almost wished we would come off. I directed from the back with my hands and the young boss shouted high-pitched, ugly words at the driver to get him to follow correctly. I thought back to earlier that day, when I had been asked if I wanted to put my money away in a security box. The girl at reception had been very emphatic about doing it in order to protect my cash, given the high crime rate that some tourists experienced. I had agreed and gave her the majority of my money.

When we arrived at the hotel, we went through the back way. Upon seeing the girl from earlier working behind the reception desk, I asked if she could retrieve my money from the cash box.

'You have no money in there, sir,' she said unconvincingly.

'Yes I do. I have money in there. You did it for me only hours ago.'

'No sir, sorry,' she said smiling.

'You have no money?' the small man said through gritted teeth with eyes as wide as the devil.

'I do. I put it here earlier,' I said emphatically.

'You come now,' he said to me in a loud voice, whilst grabbing my arm and leading me outside.

Smash! A glass bottle hit me over the back of the head as I took my first steps outside. However, the force wasn't enough to knock me out or slow me down. Instead, it induced panic and confusion.

'You get my money now!'

'Your money? I spent money there. What money of yours do you mean?' I said.

'I spent many money on girls and drink and y-a-b-b-a!' he said menacingly.

It seemed like an odd trick to try and convince me of this. I knew, at this point, that already I had managed to get myself into a typical trap and that without paying him off I wouldn't get a break. He called over the night watchman from the hotel and handed him some money, talking to him briefly. After a few seconds, the two men started to force me up the fire escape towards my room. Although I was much bigger in size and fairly well-versed in protecting myself, considering the atmosphere of this place and the stories I had heard of the corruption that went on, I felt that going along with them was the best long-term action. The Yabba was making me paranoid and, as a result, it was making me over-think and protect myself. If I had been pissed and had at least one other friend anywhere near the vicinity, I would have hit this guy until his head exploded. Part of me was exploding with anger, but the feeling was encased in solid drug fear.

The security man took out a skeleton key for my room and let us both in with a hideous smirk plastered on his face. As we walked in the room, I felt slightly more at ease seeing my possessions lying around me, but I was acutely aware that this situation could spiral well out of control.

The snake began to investigate silently around my room. He disappeared into the bathroom and I could hear things being moved around.

'What are you doing?' I asked calmly.

'Shut up!' he said violently.

He then came out of the bathroom with a modified aerosol and a thin flint from a lighter attached to the upper part of the mechanism. He lit a flame on top of the flint and fired a blast of flame, very nearly hitting my head. I quickly reached over to my acoustic guitar lying on the bed and swung it from the neck, hitting the body of the guitar on the wall behind me. Now that the guitar was in a jagged piece, I put the new weapon out in front of me and charged against his flamethrower. At that point, he took a second bottle of liquid and sprayed the contents all over the walls behind him, which blocked our exit and then pointed the spray on the wall.

'If I go, you go! The whole place goes. Understand?'

I smashed the rest of the guitar into pieces against the wall. He then suddenly lost his temper and charged to within an inch of my face and held the flame close to my eyes. I knew it was checkmate. Even if I could think of a way to disarm him safely and get out, everything of mine was here, including my passport.

'You think about police, huh?' he shouted. 'I own police! We own police! They take you and tie you up and break your babies!'

I dropped the guitar and sat on the floor, losing what fight in me I had. My heart was palpitating from the pill and the situation was dire. The man then went over to the journal desk by the TV and looked at me. He slapped down my bank card and passport. I felt completely shocked that he had somehow found my stuff, my very important stuff. I couldn't work out how he had retrieved it, but the smile across his face told me that this was a setup and not a spontaneous thing. The girl downstairs, who claimed my cash had gone, had obviously been involved in the plot. I must have been followed. The whole thing seemed so unreal.

'You'll have to wait until nine o'clock to get money,' I said in a monotone. 'I need to get the money transferred from my bank.'

'I want the money now,' he said, growling. 'Or the cops will break your babies.'

'I can't do it. The cash has gone, you have my card, and there is no cash till the morning.'

On the last note of my word, he jumped up like a madman and started attacking any personal object or material that belonged to me like a wild dog. He set fire to my shirt and watched it burn, before putting water over it to stop it going any further. Then he went and took my toiletries and chucked them out the window. Even the hotel TV got smashed in the onslaught. I watched in horror as the situation unfolded, the Yabba clearly affecting his energy and mood. Eventually, as the sun rose through the windows behind me, he started to slow and sat, cross-legged, on the floor, drinking one of the few bottles of beer from the minibar that was not broken. He took his shirt off and leant back on the foot of the bed. I could now see that a notorious gang tattoo was plastered over his back and shoulders. From the little I had heard from my friends in the camp, these were dangerous individuals.

Fire crackers started to go off in the street behind us and, as each crackle popped in my eardrums, I could feel my heart straining and my body jump. I was a nervous wreck. As 9.00 am hit we both headed downstairs in silence. He spoke to the new receptionist, who immediately gave me a phone at the bar. He handed me my bank card but kept my passport in his pocket and played pool behind me as I called my bank. He knew instinctively that I wouldn't try anything funny or put him at risk, something that he was obviously very good at detecting. Once I had painstakingly gone through the process with my bank of transferring the money, enough for his 'debt' and for me to live on for a short period, I handed the card over to him. He smiled at the receptionist as we left towards the bank and, as his sociopathic temperament had moved to a state of satisfaction, I could feel the warm embrace of exhaustion taking over me. *Soon it would be over*, I repeated to myself and I felt the anxiety fade away with every dusty step we took towards the ATM.

★ ★ ★

I awoke from a long sleep, well into the night. Outside my window I could hear the faint murmur of people striding the quiet streets. Looking out, I saw that it was almost dawn. For me, the sky is at its most beautiful when bathed in an inch of light dissecting the cold blue frosty air, signalling a new start. My mind went back to my bedroom at home, looking out my window and feeling safe in my bed, surrounded by good thoughts and peaceful silence. Despite my nostalgic thoughts, the sense of contentment was artificial and I knew that I had to fix myself before my situation became any worse. I had caused so much upset at home to my family through my behaviour, and they needed a break. I was alone, more so now than ever before.

★ ★ ★

Eleanor Rowland – 1908 paper entitled 'A case of visual sensations during sleep'.

'It often happens that dream persons issue from behind a real door, a dream hand moves along a real wall, and a dream figure sits upon the real bed. Since my vision is so accurate, I cannot reassure myself by being certain that I am asleep. Nor am I in a slumber deep enough to accept any dream that comes without comment. My reasoning powers are active at such times, and I commune thus with myself: "No one can have opened the door, for you know you locked it." "But I see a figure distinctly standing at my elbow, and it has knocked on the door twice." "You are probably asleep." "How can I be? I see and hear as distinctly as I ever do." "Why, then, don't you push the figure away?" "I will. Here I am doing it." "No – you are not doing it at all, for you can see that you have not moved an inch." "Then I am asleep after all – the figure is not there, and I need not be afraid of it.'

★ ★ ★

After a long rest, I awoke in the hotel room in the early morning. I had about fourteen hours sleep and the effect of drowsiness was taking a long time to wear off. As I stepped out of the room, the housekeeper was busy cleaning the communal area around the stairs, but she stopped what she was doing to greet me with a warm smile.

She was a healthy-looking woman with Westernised features, but obviously local and Thai. Her clothes were casual and loose-fitting and her hair was tied back, revealing a slightly hot face. The pearly white teeth – which, in comparison to mine, were like snowdrops – showed a pleasant demeanour and, given the events of yesterday, it was something I wanted to be around. It's strange how something as simple as a nice smile will create such an instant opinion of someone.

'How are you?' she said. 'I remember seeing you with that boy yesterday. Not too good.'

'Yes I was, but it's all over now.'

She smiled and carried on sweeping the floors.

'I think you might want to move hotel. He is very dangerous, you know,' she said casually.

'Well, I wouldn't know where to go.'

'I can help you if you want,' she said. 'If you look after me.'

'I can sort you out,' I said, assuming a money transaction.

I felt that I could do with some local guidance and making a friend wouldn't necessarily be a bad thing.

'Ok. I'll meet you back here in one hour! My name is Lin.' She flashed another smile at me before resuming her work.

I knew I had to have a conversation with my family back home, as I believed I wouldn't survive much longer. I headed off in search of an internet café; my plan was to make a call and ask for some financial help and to perhaps see if anyone I knew was in the area on the off chance. The feeling of anxiety was still hanging over me and I was swallowing Xanax like a madman. I spent my last few notes on cigarettes and pills, the symbolism of which wasn't entirely lost on me.

★ ★ ★

Lin crossed the busy street in the upper part of town, dodging the bikes and cars as she darted towards an old, three-storey building. The building itself was worn down and grey, with rot festering on the outside walls. In the basement of the building was a small bar and pool table. A few locals buzzed around the entrance, while two Westerners played pool and sipped bottled lager. She ventured past the players and beckoned a wizened old woman sitting behind the bar to follow her into the back. As the two women brushed through the narrow walkway, a young man sloped in behind them.

'I am meeting the man to take him a hotel in half an hour?' Linn said.

'Do you have his keys for the room now?' asked the old woman.

'Yes. I have his clothes and possessions already downstairs.'

The young man pulled himself out of the darkness and revealed the serpent-shaped face that many recognised around town. It was the man from the bar, and he was far closer to the scene of the crime than anyone else would have dared to be.

'Make sure you bring him here and take his passport from him. Tell him it is for security.'

★ ★ ★

I found an internet café, just ten minutes from my hotel and feet away from the beach. The heat was so strong that it bore down on the pavements and resonated back up to my face, and I was grateful for the icy blast of air con shuffling out from the entrance. It was a small café with only two computers and a tiny reception desk at the back acting as a makeshift bar. A fat American was sitting behind the bar talking to a Thai woman over a cold beer. I approached him and asked for the use of the phone and the computer for one hour. He handed me an old white portable phone and a small stub for the computer.

I dialled the familiar number and eventually I could hear the phone ringing. With every buzz from the speaker I could feel my anxiety notching up. I didn't know who in my family would answer, and I become even more nervous as I held the battered phone.

'Hello,' my father says.

44

'Hi, it's me. I'm in Ginoh. I'm staying at a hotel nearby.'

'Ok, good. So are you staying out there for a while, then?'

'Yes. I will be. I ran into a little trouble yesterday.'

'Oh God! Typical. Well, what happened?'

'It's not that bad. I just got mugged, in a manner of speaking.'

'Well, have you been to the police?'

'No, I haven't. But it's ok now, I promise.'

'Do you need some money then?'

'Yes, I could do with some help. I will pay it all back when I'm home.'

'Well, that's fine, but stay out there and explore. Your mother and I could do with the break,' he said in a solemn tone.

I knew that my father wanted me to stay away as long as possible. It was clear to him that the chances of me changing were minimal and he just wanted the peace. After a few pleasantries he agreed to wire some money to a tourist exchange and we agreed to speak again in 'a while'. I felt the twinge of stress rise up and down through my head like electricity; despite the pain and hardship of the withdrawal and my original intention, I had managed to get into trouble already. I toyed with the idea that I was unlucky and this was something I could not have prevented, as the very thought that I had been responsible for this latest situation was too much for my mind to cope with. The denial of the drug-taking, drinking and aching to party like a wild man was brushed aside to become a lost memory. If I conceded at this point that my strategy was wrong, I would be admitting that I needed to change far more than the short physical punishment I had put myself through in the camp.

During the conversation with my father, he had mentioned that an old family friend, called Anthony Gallagher, was staying very nearby and that I might consider meeting up with him if I wanted to see a friendly face.

Anthony was a short, stout man in his late fifties. His dark, oiled hair and stocky shape fitted the image of the archetypal cockney villain. Smart Italian suits for business and leisure shirts for fun. He was the type of man who would move with minimal effort if he had to; he had been a natural fighter and amateur boxer in his younger days, but the ravages of age meant he had to leave much of the hands-on approach to the hangers-on within his remit. He'd built himself up from a working class lad in the East End to a successful property developer by the time he was thirty, and any opportunity to increase his wealth and connections was taken very seriously.

Five years previously, he had listened to a business proposal from me about a venture into the entertainment world. I had proposed putting together a weekend party at a London club and verbalised the recorded profits of similar products – which, in fairness, would be incredible if you got them right. It was estimated that you could make nearly twenty grand in one night and, worst-case scenario, you would get your money back, with the right date and the right venue. As he had just left one business and was looking for opportunities, I approached him about my venture to the tune of ten thousand pounds.

Once I had the agreement in place, I then set off to get the ball rolling with a large venue known for its weekend exuberance. My anticipation for success was unshakeable.

I approached the club's management who, at the time, owned three popular venues in London and organised a meeting at their celebrity-packed bar in Soho. My father, ever the helpful supporter of my attempted successes, came with me and sat opposite the owner and his son in the lavish art deco setting.

'Well, last year we made recorded profits of fifteen million,' the owner said with a hint of a Birmingham accent.

'That's great,' replied my father. 'Sounds like we're in the right area then! What would you say is the best thing to do with this night, to make sure we have ourselves covered?'

'You don't want to spend more than, say, eight thousand on the promotion for the first night, and that includes the DJs,' the owner said.

'That sounds like a lot of money to spend on just one night,' I said nervously.

'That's true, but you can do very well if you do it right,' he replied. 'And I'm sure we can have a fruitful relationship post event – which means more success for everyone,' he added quickly.

'Is there any security for us?' my father asked.

'I'll tell you what,' said the owner. 'If you have less than half the capacity come through the building, then I'll waive the rent.'

Shaking hands on that deal was an exciting and comforting experience. I felt on top of the world and inspired to work hard at making this a success. Both my father and I left the meeting with a firm commitment and hope for the future.

When the night came about two months later, I was a thousand pounds over budget and wired to snap at any moment. I had spent every waking hour fighting the good fight against jealous promoters, two-faced villains and a tide of stress from my worried father and my investor, Anthony. The night was successful ultimately, and we had three quarters full capacity, which was better than expected; therefore, the omens were good and, for one brief moment, I felt the weight lift off my shoulders. Unfortunately, much of the money was siphoned off by the new owners, untrustworthy cashiers and dangerous unknowns who managed to get their cut with no stress whatsoever. I was left with a massive responsibility that was killing me inside.

I didn't sleep properly for the next two months of running the business, desperately trying to make up for the losses for everyone's sake. I was in way over my head. Eventually, the whole thing came to an abrupt stop when the club was raided, rather publicly, after my third event.

As I had attempted to run the business as best I could and worked like a dog for next to nothing, it was an unspoken rule that this should be the end of the business and we would all have to wipe our hands of it. My investor wasn't happy, but he understood and moved on to pastures new. I felt that he wasn't the type of man to not want his money back, but I also knew that I didn't have any to give and hoped that the family ties and longstanding friendship would make the unfortunate news pass amicably.

* * *

As I headed off to meet Anthony at his new off-shore business – a tourist bar situated in the red light district of town – I found myself thinking of the pitfalls of meeting up with him and whether I was better off alone. The streets of the district in the day were sand-strewn and looked beaten-up. Everywhere you looked there was litter and downmarket hustlers on every corner. The Wild West didn't have shit on this place.

As I approached the bar, the first thing that caught my eye was a large drunken man sitting at the very back of the bar, half hidden by the shade and wearing scruffy clothes. Even for this area, he looked ravaged by the years and the bad mood was externalised for everyone to see. I ordered myself a drink from the nearest barmaid and slugged a double whisky with ease, taking a second glass over to the man in the darkness.

'I'm here to see Anthony,' I said.

Without saying a word, the man took a mobile phone out from his pocket and rang who I could only presume was Anthony, whilst continuing to give me a dirty look. His eyes showed menace and I could see that he was a man of no compromise. Although his shabby exterior matched the surroundings, he showed me that he personally was a physical threat.

After a few minutes I felt a tap on the shoulder. Turning around, I saw the man himself, dressed in shorts and designer summer shirt. He didn't look angry, but he wasn't looking happy – a perfect antithesis of a poker face.

'Long time no see!' he reeled off.

'Yeah, I know. It's been a while,' I said.

'You been avoiding me?' he said suggestively.

I could feel the drink in my hand becoming heavier and the heat was making me drip with sweat underneath my unsuitably heavy clothes.

'No I haven't. You know that.'

'Well, it's been nearly five years and I haven't seen my money.'

'But you know I tried my best with that business,' I said. 'It's always a risk in business.'

'Don't give me that. I think you either spent all the money yourself or it went up your nose. I've been there myself, so don't kid a kidder.'

'I'm not trying to. I did everything right, but I was in over my head. I couldn't stop the shit happening around me.'

I could see him wavering as to whether to continue the conversation and I saw, for the first time, that things I thought were left in the past where clearly still in the present. At least in his mind.

'Well, what about the money?' he said.

'Look, the other businesses back home are doing ok now. I'm sure I can get something sorted.'

He started to look more comfortable with the conversation and took the last statement as an end to the subject. After a lengthy pause, he took his sunglasses off and looked into my eyes with intensity.

'I will make a phone call and get back to you,' he said as he handed me a card with a number on it.

'Ok, I'll wait for you then.'

With that, he put his sunglasses back on and strode off

up the street without saying another word. I pensively sat on the nearest bar stool and pondered what was going on in his head. The one thing I had learnt from the years gone by is that the most dangerous people will never let you know what their real intentions are. Often, the quietest ones are the most dangerous, as the saying goes, but it's the ones who act the complete opposite of their true feelings who can be the most lethal.

A sociopath's defining feature is they have no awareness of other people's feelings, making it common for sudden rage and acts of violence to be committed. They often appear abnormal to those around them. A psychopath, however, will not hesitate to kill you if you are in their way, but they will plan every little detail and mimic an understanding of your emotions so that you could never tell how disturbed they actually where. I felt that Anthony fell into both categories in some ways, because he had been known to fall into rages quickly and act on impulse in many situations, but when he really held a grudge you wouldn't know anything. With drug taking, I found that my personality started to change and become more deceptive and hostile; I was more prone to anger and irrational judgements, but I knew where to draw the line, despite some terrible behaviour on my part. I always felt that I knew who and what I was about, deep down.

The fat man sat staring at me and looked deeply unhappy. He would occasionally pick up his beer, showing the extensive fat under his arm and the sweaty pits staining his t-shirt.

'What's your problem, mate?' I said.

'You think you can come in here and start giving it the

big I am, hoping for a friendly outcome,' the fat man drawled.

'Well, no. I am not trying anything. I've known the man for a long time.'

'Yeah, well you owed him quite a bit of money for a long time.'

'What do you know about that?' I said, feeling my anger rising up.

'That you've owed him money for five years and not paid it back,' he said smirking.

'Actually, it was a business that didn't pan out.' I stopped myself saying anymore. I could feel the interaction becoming a waste of time.

At that moment, the fat man's phone rang and, after a few garbled words, he handed it to me. As I put the phone to my ear I imagined that this was certainly going to be Anthony and it couldn't be good. If he didn't want to even come back and waste any time talking to me face to face, then the omens were bad.

'Listen,' said Anthony. 'I've just got off the phone with someone in England and they're saying you ain't going to pay me back. So why don't you just fuck off for now, hey!'

'Who would have said that?' I said in a staccato pattern.

At that moment the phone went dead. I handed it back to the fat man, who suddenly appeared very happy. He knew it hadn't gone well by the look on my face. I picked up my drink and charged it back, slamming the glass down on the table and giving the fat man a hissing smile. As I felt the alcohol whistle through my teeth, the fat man's smile dissipated into a grim reminder of his former self.

Lin was waiting with a wide smile as I approached the

hotel and I could see my bags had already been brought down. On one hand I was happy that I didn't have to do any more running around tidying up the room, packing cases and sorting clothes, but I also felt that I didn't know her well enough for her to go through my things without permission. My emotions were levelled out and a smile was going to be impossible, but a pleasant demeanour was possible. She greeted me with a kiss and I reacted with a hint of shock, as it seemed unusual.

I spent the journey over to the new hotel deep in thought, treading through the meeting with Anthony until it made more sense. As an over-thinker, I often would spend hours, maybe even days, obsessing about what the other person may be thinking after an event. When I was young I would be obsessed about whether people liked me; when I was a teenager, I obsessed about whether people thought I was cool and good-looking while, as an adult, it was whether people were going to cause me trouble.

The new hotel was a guest house when we arrived and I was dubious about the place from the off. The bar downstairs was like an open-air saloon and the women behind the bar could have easily auditioned for any one of the zombie horror movies that get made every year. It was a bad start and an unwelcome addition to my stress list.

'I'm not sure about this place, Lin,' I said quietly.

'You'll be fine,' she said, smiling. 'These people are the friendliest around. They are my friends and you will save money here.' She squeezed my shoulder reassuringly.

'I don't know. This doesn't feel exactly like that.'

'I am telling you. This is the best place for you right now, especially after what happened with the man and your money. You need to be here,' she said convincingly.

'Well, you may know these people, but I don't. I don't even speak Thai.'

'Ok.' She paused and placed her fingers over her mouth. 'I will stay with you.'

'You'll stay with me?' I said with increasing interest.

'You *are* a gentleman, aren't you?'

'Yes, of course,' I said, without missing a beat. I could see from the tiny fragments of fervour in her eyes and the twinkling smile that she would be more than a friend if I wished. I couldn't understand the sudden attraction she seemed to possess for me and assumed it was not legitimate, but I wasn't concentrating that hard on analysing her, or anything else for that matter. If she wanted to find a weakness in me, then she had certainly succeeded.

As I lay that night next to Lin, putting aside commonsense and anxiety for a few happy hours, two men were meeting not far away to discuss the future. Despite having no knowledge of this event, I would be the focal point.

★ ★ ★

As the needle pierced my skin into the fading red scar located directly behind my right elbow, the jolt of crystal meth hit me immediately before even a drop of blood showed in the canister. As Lin gently pulled back the plunger, the rush of blood swirled and darkened inside the syringe and I felt the cold rush of the drug rise up from my throat and cause an involuntary cough. As she slammed the drug into me, I could only hear a whining sound and my eyes shuddered, as the fragments of chemical rolled up into my brain with a heavy push from the heart.

MY STATEMENT:
Earlier that day, Lin had suggested that we have a few drinks and spend the day in bed. The idea seemed easy and fun and I had enjoyed a very lazy afternoon. We drank whisky and had ice cold beers from fridge in the room. As the evening approached, we had grown tired and drunken from the day's activities and Lin said that we were wasting our free time, slouching in bed. I myself have always felt that, if I am in bed with a woman and we can watch trashy films, eat food and drink alcohol, then I will be a contented man.

The subject of drugs had come up and Lin said that she could get 'Ice'. I said I was in no position to spend so much money, as it could cost up to two hundred pounds a gramme at home. She told me this was the crème de la crème and it would cost a fraction of the price. The idea of doing ice with this new stranger in bed, paying peanuts for it and not even having to leave the room to get it, was too much of a temptation.
END OF STATMENT

Two days had passed since finding a source of very strong crystal meth 'ice', and I was incredibly dehydrated and strung out. I had been back to the internet café to speak with my father again to ask for money and I was finding it very hard to keep my memory in check. My father helped me, but I was very aware of the tone and disappointment in his voice.

'I'm sorry to call again, but I need some more money,' I had said. 'I need to pay for the hotel for some more nights and I have bills, but I don't know how many. Can you please just help me and we'll sort it out when I get back?'

'This is getting stupid! Where is all the money going and why are you speaking like that?' he said in an alarmed voice.

'I don't know what to say. I'm not too well at the moment.'

'Well, you better make this last and don't call again for a while.'

Through the drug haze I could still sense the massive disappointment and I felt sad for the both of us. I started to feel that the withdrawal in the camp was a distant memory, but the ice in my brain was telling me that I was okay because I wasn't doing heroin any more.

For anyone who knows about narcotics, the key thing about crystal meth is that it will have you broken down in a world of your own quicker than any other drug. It may not be physically addictive, but the mental addiction is so strong that you will never want to stop the high, not even for a day or a night. You can start out as a smartly-dressed intelligent person completely on the ball, but within a few weeks of use you will be underweight, dressed in torn and dirty clothes, unaware of true reality and on the point of entering psychosis. It truly is hell on earth. The only reason that people abstain from it in some places more than others and restrict their descent and destruction is because of price, something that is controlled by the powers that be, and is a clear example of corruption in the war on drugs.

As I lay in bed with Lin, sweating and obsessing with paranoid thoughts, I could see the little bags of meth lying around the room. Pyrex pipes lay strewn on the bedside cabinets amongst the syringes and spoons and I felt truly disgusting. I couldn't bear the idea of doing anything at that point and I felt that everyone outside of the room was a potential threat. I couldn't separate the reality from the unreality and I knew that something was wrong, I just couldn't put my finger on it.

'Lin, I think someone may be after me. I don't know why, but I'm worried about it,' I said quietly, in case someone was listening outside the door.

'Why would someone be after you?' she said, smiling menacingly.

'I'm not sure. I think something happened a few days back with someone that I...' I was cut off before the sentence could finish.

'Know? No darling, you don't know anyone here, but I did meet some man by the hotel who was looking for you.'

'What kind of man?'

'A big black guy, very angry face,' she said quickly.

'What? That sounds weird. I don't know anyone who...' She cut me off again.

'He said you were in trouble.'

'Why didn't you tell me before?'

I jumped up off the bed and went over to the hotel

door, which I immediately chained and double-locked. I could feel the sweat pouring off me and shivers ran up and down my spine. I took the sticky fire warning label and placed it over the peephole in the door. My breath was shallow and constant, my heart was palpitating beyond belief and I felt like my brain was being zapped by invisible rays every second. I took a glass of water from the side and slugged it back, starting to feel the incredibly dry, carpeted feeling on my tongue. In the mirror and I could see the dark circles under my eyes and the dry purple hue to my lips. I started to scratch my arms and see the marks and feel that, somehow, the little hairs were moving.

As I scanned the room, everything seemed different and smaller. The smell was bad in the air and the floor seemed incredibly dusty and dirty. Lin lay there on the bed, watching me squirm and worry, whilst lighting the encrusted drug in the pipe to get a few more hits. Finally, I pushed the dresser along the squealing floor towards the door of the room; despite its heavy weight, my fear pushed the thing tight and secure. With a few breathless steps back to the bed, I crashed down and passed out. As the room began to disappear and sleep began to embrace me for the first time in nearly three days, I could see Lin sitting upright against the bed tapping away at her phone. My last thoughts were that, despite my fading sanity, I knew that something was amiss with this woman. I just didn't know what.

★ ★ ★

I woke up after a heavy spell of unconsciousness with the

sunlight streaming through the window onto my face. I could feel the encrusted eyelashes sticking my eyes together and my tongue was swollen and painful. I could feel an ache in my throat and a constant tingling feeling whenever I breathed, which forced me to take shallow breaths. I sat up and held my face in my hands, waiting for my brain to switch on.

I need to get to a doctor, I thought to myself. I was in a lot of pain and I could barely move. However, I didn't know how to even organise something like that, and I didn't know what the hell I was going to do.

I looked at Lin sleeping in the bed. I didn't want to wake her. The uncomforting way in which she handled me the night before made me think that she secretly hated me, for reasons I didn't understand.

'Ow!' My throat was killing me and there was a ringing in my ears. *This must be bad,* I thought. I continued to worry and stress, focusing on more internal problems.

On the floor I could see my boxer shorts, jeans, and t-shirt. They must have smelt bad but, in the current state I was in, there was no way in hell I was going to sniff the material first. As I half-heartedly put my clothes on, the first thing I noticed was that the t-shirt was wet. Then I saw, right next to the pile of clothes on the floor, a half empty bottle of whisky and guessed that the wetness was caused by clumsy drinking. As my self-hatred increased ten-fold, the reality and pain became almost unmanageable and I collapsed on the floor with a thump.

While I reeled in and out of audible sounds and blurry visuals, I could vaguely see Lin running around me and collecting clothes and checking me for what I could assume where vital signs. Although I didn't speak any Thai, I could tell that she was frantic. I took this as a sign that something would be done and let my brain pass out.

The next time I opened my eyes I was in a hospital bed surrounded by other sick patients in a large temporary room. The change of scenery was a shock, but I noticed straight away that my mouth wasn't so painful and I felt slightly calmer. I looked up and saw two large drip bags that were filtering liquids into my arm; I tried to make out what the ingredients were, partly to ascertain what was wrong with me and partly to see if I was being given anything good. The fact that my mind was quick to think such thoughts, given the gravity of my possible situation, caused me to feel sad for myself and completely aware that my drug situation was even worse than before. How could I have allowed myself to get so fucked up so quickly?

On the other side of the room I could see a police officer, still dressed in uniform, lying on a bed with drips feeding him from above. He was moaning in agony and I could see that his arm was bleeding and, despite the bandages, was clearly in a bad way; his jacket had been almost ripped apart at the shoulder to get to the wound. I took a guess that he had been shot or stabbed, but couldn't be sure. The thing that shocked me was that this man, who was obviously in such a serious state, had no one helping him and that he was in some way considered to be in less need of help than me, an idiot who had overdosed on amphetamines. It made me feel sick to my stomach and ashamed, and I somehow knew that I wasn't over the worst of it.

★ ★ ★

I arrived back in the guesthouse and headed upstairs to my room. It was always a struggle getting to the top of the building, with creaky staircases and certain floors littered with old furniture. The darkness often made people lose their footing as they travelled up and, in my state of weakness, I tripped on almost every step. If anyone were to have seen the ascent they would have assumed I was injured in some way, or mentally disabled. Given my recent actions and the state of my head, I was beginning to assume I was mentally disabled anyway, so a few lurkers in the dark casting aspersions on my character were the least of my worries.

I decided that I would have to return home. This could not get any better and, despite the ill feeling my family might have towards me, they would not want me to die out here, which was exactly how I predicted this adventure would end. My gut instincts had always played a major part in keeping me safe from various life-threatening moments in my life, but up till now I always depended on the kindness of my family and friends to help me when I couldn't help myself. Years of selfish behaviour had pushed people's kindness to the edge and now I was in a situation that my instincts told me was far from over.

As I entered the room, I noticed that most of my clothes had gone missing, as had my boots. Checking around the room, I could see that very little was left of my possessions, a fact that made me feel far more nervous about trying to leave. The suitcase was still in the corner but, apart from an airplane travel magazine, it was empty.

The only measure I had taken to ensure I wasn't left high and dry was to always keep my money in my jeans pocket. I pulled out the remaining roll of notes and counted through in silence, looking around every so often at the door. Anyone creeping up the decaying staircases would have given themselves away, while anyone hiding in the shadows somewhere on the top floor would have made a sound at some point. My mind was razor sharp at that point for any unusual activity. I was putting myself on Def Con 5 and I wouldn't be lowering it until I had got far away from this place.

I sat on the edge of the bed, observing the noise and bluster in the streets below, thinking of everything and nothing. Loneliness and loss were recurring themes in my head and I felt very different, sitting there with my problems. In the past, I had become ingenious at solving problems, even in the worst situations and state of physicality, which was probably the reason I had carried on such an extreme lifestyle for so long.

A memory suddenly came to me of when I was nineteen years old. I was in a situation I had deemed hopeless with no end in sight. I had been partying at a friend's house in central London, with lots of wealthy sons and daughters of important people buzzing in and out of a Brompton Road address. I had found myself at that time to be unable to carry on such an exuberant lifestyle with my peer group and decided that I would deal cocaine at the party and reward myself with the powdered credits. I knew the entire night that something had changed in the dynamic between my so-called friends and I, with people only talking to me to obtain cocaine and many promising imaginary funds.

I had spent the night using large amounts of the drug and retaining no money whatsoever, as well as the ever increasing realisation that I was a shadow on the peripheries of this upper class group of friends. Any sign of my intellect and personality was washed away in a sea of bad memories and flaky friends and I knew that this weakness for popularity would be my undoing. The next day, I had spent many hours sitting in the ebbs of a dated party, with no more than twenty pounds in my wallet to show for it. The depression was the main enemy of creation in this scenario; wallowing in a sea of remorse and not getting into action.

Eventually, when I had less than three hours left to pay a small-time psychotic dealer his bailed funds, I drove my beat-up car down to a friend of a friend and sold it for a few hundred pounds and begged for mercy at the hands of the drug peddler to give me time to come up with the rest. It was the most painstaking, endurance-testing and depressing weekend of my life and, when I arrived home and saw my Mum, I broke down in tears and couldn't stop for the rest of the night. Some tough guy wheeler dealer I turned out to be.

Lin came up and opened the door. I could only see her from the edge of my vision and she was silent for a good few minutes. It was a silence that you could feel, uncomfortable and penetrating.

'So, are you better now from the hospital?' she said.

'You mean did I get better at the hospital?' I said, trying to be difficult for the sake of it.

'Yes.'

'Yes, I did,' I replied after a pause and with slow annunciation.

The atmosphere was frosty and she knew that I had twigged something was not right in the state of Denmark. Even I knew very little about what was going on, but the different sides I had seen of Lin in such a short space of time, and the lack of shock at the recent situation, showed me that there was more to her than met the eye. I could feel the heat of anger building up inside my head and irritation at the pseudo quality of her emotions.

'I'm leaving tomorrow,' I said firmly.

'Why?' she said quizzically.

'Because I have to get home for work.'

She paused and thought rather obviously, twirling her ankle on its axis so that her foot rocked back and forth. She did not speak again for a few minutes.

'You have paid the bills, then? And my money?' she said coldly.

'What bills? And what do you mean your money? You stayed with me in my rooms, you used my money for drugs and drink and food.'

'I stayed with you for nearly a week now.'

'So you're charging me for sex? Is that it? In fact, honey, I think I should be charging you.'

'No, no, no! You have me stay with you and I look after you.'

'You mean, the money we discussed over finding a hotel and helping me get settled? Well, in case you hadn't noticed, I'm not exactly settled. I have no possessions left and I'm a fucking mess.'

'I have to speak to someone about this,' she said casually.

It hit me then that she wasn't open to argument and

64

she wanted paying, regardless of my opinion or state of reality. The feeling of doom and embarrassment hit me like a sledge hammer and I was barely able to lubricate my tongue to speak another word.

I handed her the money she asked for and I stormed out of the room, heading for the streets to settle my mind on what needed to be done. In my pocket I had a tiny bag of crystal meth that had been left over from a few nights before. I darted off into a side street and crushed the insides with a card against a wall, then popped open the bag to sniff the insides as covertly as possible. The night time shade and busy street noise meant that I wasn't remotely visible, but years of practice promoted my obsessive behaviour.

Anxiety was always the key to my drug use. If I felt fear and panic creeping into my brain, I would exorcise it with drugs, and often the effect was simply to exacerbate the bad feeling. The rush and relaxation of the snort, the smoke, the push of the chemical was my real life switch for reality, but the fuse box in my mind was often very unreliable and lights would switch on and off within minutes. When the lights go out in a house, the trip to the basement becomes a lot more daunting.

I needed to think of an escape route. I was sure Lin was planning something and the bitch had my passport. The strange unit of people in the downstairs bar, who owned the guesthouse, were undoubtedly involved; I had only ever seen their disapproving gazes and shallow lips curse my appearance as I walked by them to get to the street.

I found a litter of motorbike taxis parked outside a convenience store and I approached the closest one to me.

'Can you take me to Standing Street?' I said, whilst pointing in its general direction.

'Standing Street, yes,' the man said as he kicked the bike into action.

We travelled in a dangerous circle on the main road to head towards the infamous street. The taxi driver was obviously not a big fan of the rules and refused to give me a crash hat as he lurched towards our destination, with me holding on to the flimsy back bar of the bike. Night was approaching and the hot evening air was filled with street market smells, the sound of the bike buzzing in my ear like a mosquito. My fast-paced thoughts evolved into paranoia involving innocent bystanders as we travelled through the streets, believing that people were in 'the know' about the plan to sabotage me. The meth, combined with the situation, was bringing on signs of psychosis in my ravaged mind, something that all drug users feared more than anything.

I paid the taxi driver and headed into the pedestrian-only entrance to Standing Street. It was filled with tourists and was so noisy that it was difficult to hear my own thoughts, a possible plus in my current state of mind. The image of hope in my mind was the bulletproof vest I had seen when I first arrived in Ginoh. Despite the enormous stupidity of even needing such a thing, it seemed like an excellent idea to compensate for the level of threat I imagined; I thought it would be a secret secondary option hidden underneath my clothes. If, during my attempt to recover my passport from the bar, they tried to attack me, I'd at least be well-protected.

I saw the mounds of weapon stalls increasing as I

headed into the darker territory of the street and could feel my eye drawn to the tasers and various implements that adorned the shelves. I didn't want to become the aggressor in this mission and I felt strongly that the unknown was far more elusive, given that I was outnumbered and in a lawless area for the most part; therefore, I would only be looking for some form of self-defence in a worst-case scenario. It crossed my mind that I should be thinking of a strategy to get my incredibly important documents back, but I assumed that conversation was far too simple. I wished I was drunk instead of high. The boozy fumes of clarity that would cause me think slow and courageous would have been far more useful than the tinny, electro pop fizz that was making spaghetti of my common sense.

★ ★ ★

Two storeys up, in a gentleman's club above Standing Street, a man in a silk bathrobe was lamenting on an innocuous thought and a large cigar. Anthony was always a man of theatricality and tonight was no different to any other, with no less than four Thai hookers spread across a personal performance space, with a balcony overlooking thousands of tourists. As he lifted a short knife topped with Bolivia's finest to his ruddy potholed nose, he flipped through numerous text messages on his cell phone. His thoughts were clear but lined with malice, his acquaintances dumb to any thought in his or their own heads and a motto of revenge running heavily under cap.

Two years to the day, Anthony had held a barbecue at

his home in the leafy suburban part of south-west London, inviting a few well-known friends and family for a bit of homespun pride on a sizzling grill. The garden was large and traditional, with Victorian-style wooden benches, a dusty old workman's shed covered in vine and a large patio area for social occasions just like this one. Twenty people lined the garden eating sausages and drinking Pimm's, the sound of inane laughter and witty banter striking the air. The sun was hot and the atmosphere jovial, allowing everyone to take a day off from reality and bask in the rigmorale of an upper middle-class summer.

'So, if you don't mind me asking, David,' asked Anthony nonchalantly, 'what has happened to the business?'

'It's over! At least, I thought it was,' replied my father, slightly confused. 'It's been six weeks since I was told it was the end.'

'And the money has gone? Finished?' Anthony asked while turning a sausage.

'Yes. He tried to make it work for as long as possible, but it looks as if it wasn't meant to be.'

Anthony grimaced at the barbecue while David looked at his back. The silence was panned only by the faint air of burning meat and background noise. A minute passed before Anthony turned around with a sausage pinned on a cooking fork and a million dollar smile.

'Well, that's business! Nothing anyone can do about it now!' he said

★ ★ ★

The armour vest was sleeveless and light, indicating to me that it probably wasn't very secure. The main problem I could see was that the bulkiness of the camouflage material wouldn't fit under my t-shirt and I would need a jacket or something similar to cover it, being as the vest was considered to be a type of weapon in some countries. I asked the vendor for a cheap jacket and was given a horrible polyester bomber jacket with a cheap imprint of a superbike championship logo, something that looked equally out of place on me during such a hot night. I could feel the sweat pouring off me. Plus, the amphetamine in my system wouldn't hit the off switch, making me feel weak and tweaked at the same time.

I zipped up the jacket and dampened the sweat on my face with the sleeve before hailing another flimsy bike taxi back to the guesthouse. On the way back I tried to slow my thoughts in an ailing attempt to reduce the reality around me and bade time before the big showdown. I hadn't eaten any food in days and my blood was thin and weak, and the sweat beads from my forehead stung my eyes like acid. Despite my ample frame and height, I had lost a lot of weight very quickly and water hydration had been temporarily replaced with alcohol. The only form of nutrition I'd had was during my short stay at the hospital.

The bar came into view from my right. The lights were on and I could hear music. As we got closer, I noticed there were two motorbike taxi men on the other side of the road. They were wearing fully-closed helmets and their brake hands seemed to be covered by something. As my bike started to pull in and brake, I could clearly see that they had one hand tied inside a plastic bag, while the accelerator hand was gloved. The mystery of the plastic bag was the only thing I could focus on as I got off the bike and paid the driver. The motorbike riders tilted their heads in my direction and followed me as I entered the bar. Behind the bar were the old wizened woman and Lin, both smiling and obviously very disinterested in me.

A few of the prostitutes were wandering around the bar together, as if in a pack. This seemed unusual to me, as the bar was for tourists only and they were often shouted at in Thai if they ventured too close or tried to procure business. This time, however, there was no shouting and they obviously felt comfortable enough to sit near the pool table and walk around, talking amongst themselves. Some of these prostitutes were undoubtedly lady boys, but in Thailand it's difficult to ascertain which are which without some serious scrutiny. They even have beauty contests in which male and females compete against each other, the winner nearly always a post-op. Alexei, from the camp, explained to me in graphic detail how, because it was so difficult to tell, he would perform a test in which he would stick his hand down their underwear and feel to see if they were wet; it was a test that, despite the modern technologies like lubricants, you just can't fake.

The atmosphere was, at first glance, jovial, but I instinctively felt an undercurrent of hostility. I believed, for the first time, the drug that was coursing through my veins was finally keeping me alert in the right away. I ordered a large double whisky and slugged it back, feeling the harsh vapour of alcohol rush down my parched throat, an unpleasant and vicious feeling. I noticed that someone was walking up the wooden step towards my part of the bar, but I kept my eyes fixed on the glass, thus I had no perception as to who it was.

I felt a hand on my shoulder and I turned, too slowly, to see the man from the bar who had robbed me. His dark, shark-like eyes stared at me with no trace of distinguishable emotion and the panic and fear I had felt that night came flooding back in waves of pain. He was holding a pair of long scissors, which were extended over the edge of the bar and, as his eyes caught mine eyeing the metal, he began to smile an ugly smile.

'What are you planning to do to me?' I said quietly.

'You owe me more money,' he said, squeezing my shoulder.

'What do I owe you money for?'

'For staying in this town, for favours. You know.'

I could see the old woman in the bar smiling a wrinkly, evil smile, with dark menace in her eyes and I cursed the fact that my paranoia had actually been based on reality. The bikers were still pointing their plastic bags directly at me and I took a wild guess that they were concealing guns.

'Tell me,' I said confidently, 'do they have the guns inside those bags to stop the shells hitting the ground?'

'Yes! You know about this!' He laughed and seemed genuinely impressed by my knowledge.

'You think you need this for me?' I said, keeping my eyes straight ahead.

The man got up and left the bar stool, sticking the scissors inside his back pocket and wandering over to the bikers. No one at the bar attempted to interact with me, and not even a glance was passed my way. The man headed back over to me, but he didn't sit on the bar stool. I felt a twinge in my back as the rusty scissors were pressed hard in between my shoulders, the shock making me judder and push my glass over the edge of the bar. An old mobile phone was dropped over my right shoulder on the bar in front of me.

'You call whoever you can and get money sent,' he said.

'What money and where? It's a different time zone in England!' I replied, starting to panic.

'And you come out back and take this jacket off!' he said loudly.

'Why take the jacket off?'

'Because you have vest on. We know you bought this.'

He grabbed my jacket and tugged me off the bar stool, causing me to nearly trip. I headed off round the back of the bar, past the rickety stairs and under the small rotting door that hid the yard used for storage and valuables. I unzipped the jacket and felt the cold air of the night hit my sweat-soaked front, the sensation making me feel surprisingly relaxed as I unveiled my armour vest. It was almost as if I was accepting my fate and I was too tired to care anymore.

I handed the man the vest and I put back on a sweaty, cheap t-shirt, while he surveyed the material and attempted to pull the armour plates from inside the casing. As he led me back out into the bar, I could feel the scenery around me blurring and I wanted the steps to last a little longer, because I knew that what lay ahead was uncharted territory.

As the night wore on, I had asked for a piece of paper and a pen so that I could buy some time to think of a way out of the situation, pretending that I needed to write down the names of people who could help. I kept thinking that this would be a difficult place for him to kill me, especially with a gun and to have no questions asked. You would need to have money to cover something up and have invented alibis with the police. Maybe I just didn't realise how lawless the place was, or how much crime was committed on a daily basis; perhaps I was just blind to how easy this actually would be.

I beckoned over the man, who was chatting casually to the bikers on the other side of the bar.

'I'm ready to call someone, but I need to know how much!' I said.

He pulled out a piece of paper and settled it in front of me on the bar. I could see that it contained bank codes for an account and, despite the occasional bit of Thai written down that I couldn't understand, it was obvious what the various number sections were. Written in blue pen at the top of the page was a pound sign and, next to it, the number '15,000'. He pointed at the number and my face fell, knowing instantly that this was no 'boy scout' gang, and the probability of me getting this money was zero. I picked up the phone and dialled my parents' home number, hoping for a miracle.

* * *

As the phone rang, the only other sound I could hear was my thumping heartbeat.

'Hello,' my father said wearily.

'It's me. I'm in a really bad situation and I need you to listen and help.'

'What the fuck do you mean? Do you know what time it is?'

'Yes. I didn't want to call but I had to. I'm being held by these people and they want money.'

The silence said everything and I didn't take a breath the entire time.

'Well, this sounds like bullshit!' he said angrily. 'You aren't getting anything!'

'I know you think you know what is going on, but you don't! This is real. My life is in danger. I'm being careful about what I'm saying because they are around me.' I could feel the anger towards my captors rising as I realised I was making my father more and more annoyed.

'How much are you talking about?' he said quizzically.

'Fifteen thousand.'

'Fifteen thousand what?'

'Pounds!'

The phone rustled and went dead. I kept the handset to my ear and sat very still, not acknowledging what had just transpired. I could feel the eyes of the man staring at the side of my face, and the slight burst of pride and anger I'd felt a few seconds earlier had started to dissipate into fear and isolation. My ears felt numb and sore and my eyes were watery and tired, a combination that indicated I had no intoxicants or natural energy sustaining me. I could feel tears starting to stream out of my eyes, and the sound of them hitting the alcohol-soaked wood on the bar made the rat-faced scissor man laugh and snigger. He didn't even bother to ask about the call; instead, he walked over to the other side of the bar towards the bikers. I felt as if my time was up and sat pathetically on my bar stool, in my rotting clothes, feeling very sorry for myself. I tried to imagine what the gunshot would be like and if I'd feel any pain.

A last stab of adrenaline and self-preservation hit me like a thunderbolt and I stood up slightly from my stool. The bikers noticed and made jerky movements with their bodies, rustling the bags and maintaining their control. The rat-faced man pulled the scissors out from his pocket and ran back across the bar towards me, sensing that I may be trying to escape. I waved my arms emphatically above my head to indicate that I simply had an idea. The man reached me and stuck the scissors into my side, lightly cutting the skin and causing an instant cramp in my solar plexus.

'Look. I can ring someone I know and they can get money,' I said.

'Who is this?' he said, pulling the scissors away.

'My ex-girlfriend. I can call her and get money.'

'You call then. But no funny business.'

I called my ex-girlfriend's number quickly and prayed she would answer the phone. I knew that, if I could get her on the phone, I could indicate she should play along and that it would buy me some time. It wasn't like she would have the money, but it would be a good start and I couldn't think of anyone else to ask. If it failed, then I would have no more options.

★ ★ ★

As the morning light began to fill the streets outside the bar, I could see no one and hear nothing. My captors had dwindled down to just the old woman and the rat-faced man, who had been ignoring me for some time. Tears stained my eyes and my mouth tasted like rotting meat, while the bumps in my arms caused by needle misses pulsated like putrid bombs.

As the exhaustion fell deep into my body, my two remaining captors left the bar without a word. I had been left alone, completely alone. The thought rolled in my mind that this was very strange and that I must be free, yet the menace of doomed fate still kept me planted on the bar stool. My heart began to ache from the palpitation and I twisted the question over and over in my brain as to whether I should move or stay still. It could be my last chance of escape and, however unusual it was, no better scenario could be presented. It just seemed so odd that everybody had appeared to have gone and that I was given this option. Or perhaps it wasn't an option? Perhaps my movement would be met with quick execution, with no evidence of any wrongful person to blame. The police would probably take the view that I was a drug user, without documents or possessions, and somehow I had met my fate randomly at this point.

I turned my head and saw a group of monks walking past the bar. I was too scared to speak and too tired to move or think, yet the image filled me with a temporary calm. It was Sunday now and the monks would be collecting donations and offering help, a regular activity in this part of the world. The monks turned and looked at me, while I sat like a statue and said nothing. The air was so quiet you could hear a pin drop at ten paces. This gaze went on for many minutes and the only communication we had was through a distant observation. When they turned and left the bar, I wondered whether I should have asked them for help, but the fear of Holy men seeing me in this state made the move impossible. It created a sense of shame that I bottled away for another time.

★ ★ ★

I hung off the edge of the bar's entrance. The rickety wood before the dusty ground was seemingly impenetrable and I had successfully created an invisible wall of solitude. It would be wrong to say I had created this solitude, as it was clear that my captors had used quite intense behaviour to create a sense of fear, the most powerful emotion a human can use to control, unless you count love. I think fear and love, to a certain extent, are extremely similar and you can't have one without the other.

The temperature was extremely hot and I was dehydrated beyond belief. My diet of alcohol and chemicals in hot temperatures meant that my body fat had decreased by about thirty per cent, which was probably why so many famous and not so famous perpetrators of this lifestyle continued to see benefits. The old t-shirt I wore had dried out, but even I could smell it through the stuffy nose and smog fumes wafting around the town. Looking around, I could see literally no one and my paranoid mind started thinking crazy thoughts about death and reality, and where mine would meet its end.

I finally pushed myself with reinforced logic about how to survive hostage scenarios in which it was always advisable to take any opportunity to leave and not to think twice. My mind kept pushing back against logic and told me I would be shot or arrested, and that no hope was waiting for me. I thought of England and my home and how I had everything, wanting so desperately to go back in time and reverse the misbehaviour. It occurred to me that you really don't appreciate things quite for what they are until they are taken away from you.

I stepped off the porch and headed slowly for a different part of town, frantically swivelling my paranoid head side to side looking for assassins and enemies. I could feel the hot earth under my feet, while the sun reflected its humidity onto my now frail body. With fragility, your body can only feel love as hate becomes an impossibility. When you're high on certain stimulants you might feel love and empathy because your brain is taking a bubble bath and sipping on champagne, but when your body is empty and battered the brain is stuck in a cold dark prison cell, regretting and hoping for survival.

I reached a McDonalds about two hundred yards from the bar, the familiar logo filling me with comfort and warmth. Given the hatred and criticism I might normally fire at the place, and the weak plasticised degradation it makes me feel back at home, this was a startling contrast. Inside the restaurant, I saw a group of American men standing at the till talking and I immediately felt an extra burst of confidence. They were young and kitted out with matching t-shirts, denoting that they were military in some way. I went up to the men and tapped the nearest on the shoulder.

'I'm sorry to bother you, but I am in need of help,' I said through dry lips. 'These people have held me hostage and they have my passport and I don't know what to do.'

The men looked me up and down and I suddenly realised that I probably looked like every charlatan who does this kind of speech for money. I stupidly turned my arms to look at my forearms, while pondering the perception I must have given, and saw the pin marks and general dirty state of myself. The man I was talking to also saw and turned away from me without saying a word. This was by far the most embarrassing moment I had felt in a long time and what intelligence I had told me to give it up. I could feel sweat started to emanate from my head and the faint sound of music in my ears. This seemed strange, as there was no music playing in the restaurant; it was a repetitive, fast-beating sound that appeared to me like dance music. I felt very aware of myself and my hopelessness, the feeling of madness creeping in and the only possible way forward. For a moment, I wanted to sit down and let the terror creep in my head and kill me, but a black jeep pulled up outside and I was distracted.

The jeep had blacked-out windows and the engine kept running as it sat there with no obvious passengers. I was fixated on this jeep, because the fact that no one was getting out made me very nervous. All of a sudden there was a loud bang. The noise made me cower down on the table and I was suddenly very aware of the transparent glass. I was sure the noise had been a gun and I could feel myself reaching new levels of fear. When I quickly looked around, I could see there was, in fact, no broken glass or frightened people. My mind was frantic and I couldn't work out what had happened, but then the sound fired off again: 'Bang!' This time, I saw that the jeep had backfired, the exhaust smoke changing colour briefly at the tail pipe.

This was enough to warrant leaving the restaurant and, from the looks of the staff in my direction, I decided I had better get out quickly before they called the cops.

★ ★ ★

One hour had passed since my 'escape' from the bar. I felt increasingly worried because, although I had escaped my captors, the scenario was not conducive to a full-scale escape. Also, the fact I had been left alone in that bar was very strange, to be guarded only by the sense of fear that permeated the perimeter.

I looked frantically everywhere with the speed of a bird's head and the lumbering pace in body of a domestic housecat in the hot sun. This was not a moment where I had shone, or in any way proven the power of the human spirit. I felt broken and fatigued, worse than any experience so far in my life. The sweat kept pouring out of me and the beaming sun was frying my face. Any Westerner who saw me would have been forgiven for thinking I was a lost soul trapped and belonging to Ginoh.

I searched in my head for an answer, a target and goal. I would surely die if this constant, fearful wandering would be all that I could do. I knew that I should speak to an official or someone similar, and so I set off, still travelling in a straight line from where I had started. After walking for approximately two miles, I could see that the streets were becoming cleaner and more concrete; the palm trees planted at corners and roundabouts signified a positive modern holiday destination rather than the dusty confines I had become used to.

A proper bank was in sight, complete with security guard in full regalia and marble-lined walls at the entrance. I wandered over slowly, wiping the putrid sweat away from my eyes as best I could with the dirty material clinging to my body. I felt that if I asked someone in the bank whether there was an official tourist office, the kind that dealt with Visas and lost passports, I could find my way out of this mess. The very idea that I might find some simple answer kept my heart beating, and my head cleared long enough to summon a straight face and working mouth.

As I approached the guard, I could see that his face was stone set and his eyes were narrowed and serious. In his belt I could see a gun, alongside a telescopic truncheon in the utility belt. I couldn't help but think that, if our roles were reversed and I saw a monstrosity walking towards me in the hot sun, I would have had my fingers touching the belt long before we met.

Just as I was about to step onto the sidewalk alongside the bank, I noticed two young men approaching me from the right. I stopped on the ledge and looked nervously to the right, keeping my body still while I worked out who they were. The sun shone down into my eyes, making it difficult to see.

'Excuse me, are you ok?' the voice of the first man said.

The man stepped into view and I could see he was in his late twenties, around the same age as me. He was tall and his head was on a level with mine, showing me curly black rings of hair above an olive complexion; he had an athletic body to match and was dressed in cargo shorts and t-shirt. The very sight of him was a healthy contrast to me.

'I'm Akim,' he said in a Middle Eastern accent. 'You look like you need help. What is your name?'

'I'm Oliver. I'm trying to get some help. I had my things stolen, like my passport.'

'Where you have stolen?' Akim said aggressively.

'These people in a bar,' I replied. 'They stole my passport and kept me hostage.'

'We help you go get!' he said emphatically.

'No, they are dangerous and I can't go back right now,' I said dismissively. 'I would rather find some other help.'

The other man came into view and I could see that he was equally as tall and dressed in cargo shorts and t-shirt. He was athletic, but stronger than Akim in the upper body and had a steely face, with short black hair to match. The olive skin and brown eyes initially made me assume he was Italian. The accent, however, was certainly not.

'You scared of someone here? You know we are soldiers?' the man said slowly but forcefully.

'You see this!' Akim and the other man turned their forearms over to reveal a triangular tattoo with a green insignia of the letter 'S' with a tail and star at the very end. They were identical, high-quality tattoos and both men had them on the exact same point of their arms.

'This is our sign. We are a group and fearless. No one can fuck with us! You understand?' Akim said confidently.

'What is your name?' I said to the second man, slightly unnerved by the tattoos and the aggressive stance they were taking.

'Hadar,' he said with a wry smile. 'We go now!'

They started walking, both placing their hands on my arms on either side, not quite forcing me along but suggesting with weak force. I kept silent and walked at their fast pace, back down towards the bar that I had been running away from for the last two hours. My adrenaline was now back up and running and the fear was fading in and out; somehow, the unity of these strangers was giving me unnatural strength of mind.

Despite the strange turn of events, I did not question the way things were going. This may have been something to do with the deadly low hydration levels in my body, or the 'no escape' routine I had fallen into over the last few days, peaking over the last desperate few hours of my life. I could feel the sweat and frailty rubbing against my jeans, my feet aching to the point of numbness. I knew that, when I eventually took off my shoes and socks, the carnage I would see what be something for the record books; but I continued to walk on the bloody, squelching flesh in hope of the revenge and salvation through these strong, random strangers.

When we reached the bar, I began to feel a wave of fear climb into my head and I almost passed out from the surge.

'I don't want to do this! These people are dangerous,' I said out loud, while I was escorted towards the bar.

Both men ignored me, as if I hadn't spoken at all. For a moment it seemed like one of those terrible nightmares where you can't fight back, or kick the football, or coordinate like a normal person. It seemed as if my words hadn't existed. The whole way there, they had occasionally asked to confirm where we were going; but other than that, there was no other conversation. We had marched like a group of mercenaries and the mood was only perceived by the silence.

When we eventually arrived at the bar, I could see two people now serving drinks as if nothing had occurred the previous night. The old woman from the hostage night was wiping the bar with a dirty cloth, while narrowing her eyes at our little group. She had no fear in her eyes whatsoever and her gaze made me feel smaller and smaller. I could sense that she was furious I had escaped and I half expected her to morph into a wild, snarling animal and leap across to bite my head off.

Hadar and Akim walked up to the bar and, once again, turned over their forearms to simultaneously reveal their tattoos. I kept a few feet away and I could see that, as they revealed their arms, the old woman's eyes opened and dilated, her frown turning into a forced smile. It seemed as if she recognised the sign of their tattoos and it was now stalemate.

'Where is his passport and money you took?' said Akim ferociously. The old woman jumped back a step.

'There is no money. But you can have the passport, no problem!' she said calmly.

'You have money. We know!' said Hadar.

'No, he spent and paid. No money is kept here,' the old woman replied.

The two men looked around at me with angry faces, signifying they felt I was lying and that they were betrayed by my intent. The fuzzy thinking in my head had been relying on facial expressions for the last few days, and the paranoia told me that I was getting into deeper water. It seemed that the 'money' part was the issue annoying them.

Hadar slammed his hand down on the table with gusto

and leapt to the right, marching towards the back entrance of the bar where the rickety stairs started. While Akim stood silently and calmly looking at the wall, I felt an uncertainty of the safety around me. It seemed that Akim held a higher ranking of power in their friendship and that Hadar, the bigger of the two, was the enforcer in this relationship.

As I stood there, waiting for the next event, I heard a scream followed by thumps above my head. They were coming from the room I had previously inhabited and the mixture of low and high-pitched screams made my blood curdle. Then I heard a thundering of steps down the staircase and, within seconds, Hadar was in view. When he reached me, he stood inches from my frame and stared with the cold, dead eyes of a man who had witnessed a million horrors.

'You fuck this?' he said, whilst raising his pointed finger towards my old room.

'What do you mean?' I said quickly.

'The thing. The person,' he said angrily.

'You mean Lin? The woman?'

'She is no woman!' he said, raising his voice.

At that moment, the woman in question came into view and went behind the bar, using the old woman as a type of secondary shield.

'She… is a lady boy,' Hadar said.

'No she isn't. Why are you telling me this?' I said, feeling the nausea rising in my stomach.

The next few minutes became a blur as the soldier friends shouted and argued and recovered my passport, while all the time shooting dirty looks at me as I stood in the dust, shaking. My brain was juddering like an old computer at the realisation that the woman I had spent my time and bed with was, in fact, a different type of sex. It wasn't a homophobic process that was going on, but one of horror at the thought of my gullible and insatiable behaviour. Amongst these new soldier friends of mine, who were righting the wrongs of the night, I felt like a freak.

My humble, shaking body was matched only by my fragile, distorted mind. It was a nightmare of lucidity of the worst proportions and I found it hard to take a breath. How could a man meet this woman and, in minutes alone, work out she'd had a sex change? She was so slender and female in all aspects, even down to the parts themselves. The mere thought that Hadar could have seen this so easily brought up many past nights in my mind, and I thought of the people around us who had seen my behaviour and wondered what they must have thought of me. For now, I would leave the jury undecided and keep this 'opinion' of Lin as only a possibility.

★ ★ ★

Being in repossession of my passport, I was led back to where the two men lived. We had only staggered five hundred yards from the bar before we reached their hotel. It wasn't, however, what you would call a 'hotel'.

The building was located opposite the McDonalds I had ventured into that very morning. It was a three-storey house with a concave glass entrance, the signage of which read 'Foot Spa' in Thai. The place must have been one of the cleanest I had seen in town. Venturing in through the doors, I could see at least four people either side, lying back in leather chairs, bathing their feet in stone baths. Akim turned back to me and raised a forefinger to his mouth as we crept silently through the marble-floored premises. It smelt of eucalyptus and the air-conditioned temperature soothed my senses. I was almost tempted to take my own shoes off so that I could feel the soothing temperature of the floor and feel some relief.

We climbed the stairs at the back of the building and, after three floors, we reached their room. It was a pleasant building and I hoped for some rest, despite the strange fact that this wasn't really a hotel. What I didn't count on, however, was the price you had to pay for soldiers of fortune.

Soldiers of fortune can come in many different shapes and sizes. They can originate from true horror and war, focusing on big money and dangerous objectives. Sometimes, however, they can be the runt of the litter in a big man's war, finding slithers of meat to sink their teeth into. I don't think many people who follow a life of violence set out to become just that; instead, I think it follows naturally for some, who enter a war because of desperation, to leave a war with desperation.

As I was shown inside the room they shared, I encountered a new member of their troop, a man who was introduced as 'the Doctor'. He lay on the bed, which took up most of the room, and smoked a Shisha bubble pipe whilst tapping away at a laptop computer. The Doctor was a tall, olive-skinned man with long, dark blond hair and blue eyes, the antithesis of his friends. He was bulkier-looking than the others, but the frame fitted well with the rest of him and it was obvious that he was aware of his attributes. Hanging from his neck was a silver necklace with the Star of David, a Jewish symbol, indicating that the three of them may have originated from somewhere like Israel given the accents, looks and key features I had noticed in their company.

The men began to argue as soon as we were all inside the room, and the language was thick and course, which made me feel very uneasy and slightly ensnared. I was feeling very peculiar at this stage and I looked at the cold tiled floor as the comfiest-looking bed I had ever seen, desperately hoping I could curl up and shut my eyes for just five minutes. I wanted to interrupt, but there was an air of hostility. From what I could make out, it seemed they were annoyed that I had no money on me and their gesticulations showed this quite readily.

'Could I possibly have a drink of water?' I said looking at Akim.

'You can drink from the tap,' he said quickly.

I opened the bathroom door and immediately saw a filthy sink with a used condom on the side. The smell of old sex seemed to be lingering in the air and I felt myself retch as I turned the silver tap. The feeling of hostility was so strong that I dared not even move the condom and had to be very careful to avoid it. I took some sips of water and immediately wished for more, but turned the tap off and faced the room.

'How you get money?' the Doctor asked me.

'I have to message my father on line or get to a phone,' I said slowly.

'Here, you use this!' The Doctor handed me the computer while ushering me towards the bed.

I was being watched by all three of them and, as I briefly scanned their faces, it was obvious that Hadar wanted to do some serious damage to me. I went online and onto my e-mails and, as quickly as possible, I wrote an e-mail to my father. As I was just about to send the message, Akim came down into the view of the screen and took the computer away.

'I wish to check this!' he said.

It was obvious now that these guys were not good Samaritans and they simply wanted to get paid for helping me. Luckily, the e-mail was simple and it said that I needed money and pleaded not to make things difficult. I did think, however, that my life somehow was in the hands of the return e-mail that would grace their computer screen, and the fear of harm from the night before returned, striking painful aches in my chest like a morbidly obese man suffering from angina. I knew then that I had to rest if I wanted to survive. If I was to have any sense of mental cohesion and physical endurance, then I needed rest.

'May I rest for a few moments?' I asked the group.

'You need to shower!' the Doctor said fiercely.

'Could I just rest on the floor?' I asked again.

'No! You go take shower,' he said and waved his arm towards the bathroom.

I sensed that my state must have offended their senses, but I wondered if it was perhaps a religious sensibility that made them demand cleanliness from a person, especially a stranger. I felt slightly aggrieved at this; it was as if they saw me as an inanimate object rather than a human, with my integrity shot and nowhere left to turn or negotiate. For now, however, I would shower and follow their instructions, choosing safety over pride. It just wasn't worth getting killed over a little bit of soap.

★ ★ ★

As darkness of the night once again swamped the dusty town, I was washed and slightly refreshed, but terrified of my fate, as I was still awaiting the e-mail that could seal me into an early death or prolong my options for escape. The Doctor had told me we would visit a restaurant they go to and get some food which, given the circumstances, was the nicest thing to have happened to me in a week and I certainly wasn't going to argue.

When we reached the restaurant through the busy steam-filled back streets, it was obvious that this was a local venue for locals. No English translations, no Western-styled food or drink, and no walls – just a large marquee that guarded the customers from possible rain, although at this time of year only humidity would persist. It was packed with Thai people who noisily ate their way through soups and bowls of rice with meat as quickly as the food could be fried up on the cookers.

We sat down at the nearest table and, within a minute, my new captors had ordered some drinks in Thai. It was clear to me they were not fluent in the language, but they knew their way around. When the cold brown tea arrived at the table, Hadar poured me a glass first and encouraged enthusiastically for me to taste. I found this a little strange and contradictory, but was happy to keep on hydrating. He then asked if he could taste it, which seemed even more bizarre as he could easily have poured another glass for himself, but given the glimpses of aggressive behaviour I had seen previously I chose not to think about it and handed him the glass. As he took a sip, he placed his entire mouth over the glass as if placing something from his mouth into the liquid, an extremely odd site indeed. He then quickly passed the glass back.

'You drink now, more. You need!' he said, pushing the glass emphatically towards me.

I drank the glass back under the watchful eye of the group and I could taste a new material, something metallic and synthetic. Perhaps it was my imagination getting the better of me, so I chose not to think too much about it as I desperately needed to relax. Relaxing wouldn't be a problem, however, because whatever was in the drink worked very quickly and very effectively and I could feel myself almost falling asleep at the table.

Once the group had finished their food, which included me just picking at the spicy Pad Thai dish, despite my previous hunger, we went back to the room. I traipsed back on my blistered raw feet with the men hoping for many hours of unconsciousness.

That night I slept on the floor on top of a large sheet, with one spare pillow and a clean towel for covering. It was the best night's sleep I'd had in years and my aching, exhausted, half-dead body washed into a sea of dreams, granting a two-finger salute to my paranoia and a hope for a lighter tomorrow.

★ ★ ★

I woke up the next morning to the sound of bickering in a foreign language. I turned my stiff neck to the left to see Hadar pushing up a ceiling tile in the room, while the other men looked on shouting and waving their arms. He pulled something into view, which I was sure looked like a firearm, perhaps a revolver, but due to the sleep in my eyes and sudden wakefulness I couldn't be sure, as I was fairly used to my mind playing tricks on me.

'Did my father e-mail back?' I asked Akim.

'Yes. He say that he don't know why you need more money,' he replied.

'Ok. I will e-mail back. It won't be a problem,' I said confidently.

I could already feel my heart beating fast and heavy with fear. The previous evening I had fallen asleep through exhaustion, the paranoia having also been sent to bed, but the hot sunshine of the new day streaming through the dusty windows of the pokey room was sobering me very quickly.

'Ok, you get dressed!' Hadar ordered.

'Are we going somewhere?' I asked.

'Yes. We go to the crocodile farm today,' Akim said whilst putting the computer away.

The word crocodile was enough to make me distrustful, but also very aware that it could have been a threat of some kind as a result of my father's e-mail they had read that morning.

'Let me e-mail first!' I said quickly.

Akim opened and plugged in the laptop and shared a glance with the Doctor, transposing hidden words with experienced eyes. I hastily e-mailed my father and used the best and most forceful plea for money I could muster, the anxiety keeping my brain alert in order to keep my chances alive. The e-mailed was checked by Akim before sending and then we carried on preparing for our trip. I felt sick to my stomach.

As we descended the stairs and exited the glass doors of the foot massage building, I knew that I had to bid for more time as I could sense horror may be on the cards. I felt my heart leaping into my mouth as two thoughts entered my head in relation to the visit to the crocodile farm. The first was that I would be fed to the crocodiles for the entertainment of my captors, the twisting, bloodied stumps of my body captured on camera to be emailed to my family. The second scenario was that I would survive the incident, minus a limb, but again pictures of me would be taken for the purpose of blackmail, in which case I would hope to survive massive blood loss and abject pain.

We approached a motorbike vendor on the east side of town, ten minutes from the hotel. The vendor, although trying to bargain heavily towards profit, agreed to let the bikes go for the incredibly cheap fee that my captors were happy with. All around me were possible escape routes – shops and offices and hotels with English translated signs. If I had been a newbie to the town, I would have surely gone for an option and asked for help, but the lawlessness that I had experienced and leaky atmosphere told me that the baked, dry streets were no saviour.

'I don't want to get on the bike. I'm not going,' I said defiantly.

'You get on this bike now,' Hadar said through gritted teeth.

'No. I don't want to,' I replied, tears welling up inside my eyes.

Hadar walked over to me and pinched my shoulder with a grip that forced me to go in his direction, unless I would consider incredible pain. We boarded the bike and all four of us accelerated off the main street on the two bikes rented from the unknowing vendor. The swaying camera on Akim's back in the distance reminded me of the metronome of execution I had created in my head. I kept thinking of crocodiles lurking in murky depths with jaws of steel waiting to pounce on uncooked flesh, the pain of which was unthinkable.

The bike continued on a long, wide stretch of petrol-ridden carriageways outlined by desert and old Western-style fruit markets, the sound of a hundred mopeds and LPG converted cars roaring alongside us like a swarm of bees. Akim was sitting on the other bike in front of us and, out of the three of them, I preferred his moderate tone and better understanding of English. I wished I was on the bike with him and not Hadar as we swung along on the ropey vehicle with nothing to hold on to but the tiny steel hand frame behind me.

We arrived in a car park after about twenty minutes of driving and drove under a giant fake crocodile skull and some Thai signs gesturing where to park. I could feel my heart jumping in my mouth and the metallic taste of adrenaline piercing my blood vessels.

'We go inside now. You give me your helmet,' Hadar said.

After packing away the helmets and heading towards the entrance gate, I noticed that the area didn't exactly look like a torture scene or a corpse drop-off; instead, it was touristy and well-presented, with tannoys and plastic signs just like in any Western amusement park. The water was green and placid and, as we walked into the main reception area, I could see that this was not quite the raw and vapid place I had been dreading. This in turn made me feel more at ease, the jangling of home-made dreamcatchers and trinkets promoting an ease of atmosphere.

'We take a picture of us,' Akim said, suddenly producing the camera and pointing towards a pray area where others were snapping away.

I sat down with the other two men while Akim readied his camera. I felt ill at ease with this request and the fact that we were posing as 'best buddies' for a snapshot. Only hours before we had been running under a strict regime of no smiles and hostile behaviour, yet now we were pretending to be best friends. Hadar even swung an arm over my shoulders. I couldn't understand why this was happening but decided I should keep my mouth shut and play along – some things are better left in the dark when you have bigger problems ahead.

We moved around the wooden bridges lining the attraction; my captors seemed genuinely amused by the sights and became more relaxed. I maintained my poker face, but all the while thinking of the reception area of the park and the very public scenario we were in. If I could somehow get help and stay out of sight long enough, then perhaps I could start a long but safe journey home. They may have my passport but this must happen to people all the time, I reasoned. Things get stolen and people still get home.

I carefully started to linger at stalls and the slow, quiet movement and shuffling of the various people created an easy way to force some distance. I allowed my captors to move a whole bridge in front while pretending to be overly fascinated with a food stall; then, when I could see a safe gap, I slowly went against the stream of people and went back towards the reception. I could feel another shot of adrenaline as soon as I turned against the tide and used it to my advantage, sliding effortlessly in between the tourists and making it impossible to be tracked.

At the reception area I frantically looked around for a help office. I found what I believed to be something of that nature to my left and walked straight in.

'Does anyone speak English?' I said.

'Yes, I do. How can I help you?' a young man said from behind the desk.

'I have lost my wallet and passport and I need to use a computer or phone, if possible,' I replied.

'You had your passport here? Losing a passport is very serious. We should call the police!' he said with genuine worry.

'Please, if you could let me use a computer,' I said quickly. 'I can then send a message and get help.'

'You sure you don't need any more help? You are welcome to use it, sir, but it is a very important document.' The kind man then gestured towards the computer.

'Thank you, but I will do this first,' I said, hoping my nonsensical logic and plan wouldn't raise any eyebrows.

I logged onto my e-mails and quickly scanned for a reply from my father. There was a reply, as luck would have it, which had come through only minutes earlier. It was clear he had recently arrived at work as the time was around nine in the morning, so he had sent an e-mail in response to mine straight away. Within the first line I read that he had transferred some money to Western Union, followed by the codes and passwords needed to withdraw. I felt a jolt of excitement and spent a minute or so deciding what to do, while jotting down the information on some paper next to the computer.

I reasoned that if I tried to disappear on my own it would be very difficult, as I had no passport, money or possessions. Despite having genuine intent, this was not my country and I couldn't speak the language, all massive precursors in finding proper help. If I went back to my captors, brandishing the account details and hoping for a deal of some kind in return for my passport, I might also be met with more captivity and probably some nasty physicality. The moments alone in the office had been the most exhilarating in days and I wished for simpler times, where boredom was actually bliss and I didn't realise how lucky I was.

I saw the men just one bridge away from the reception area and headed over to them, holding a piece of paper and a fake plastered smile on my face.

'The money is here. I have the details,' I said happily.

'Ok. This is good,' Akim said whilst gazing around.

It seemed odd that they weren't too bothered about the money and I wondered why they weren't questioning me as to where I had gone.

'We go back to town now and later we get money,' Akim said.

The men walked out in front of the reception area

without saying another word, while I followed without question, this unexpected reaction causing total numbness. We headed back to Ginoh on the squealing motorbikes, my hands barely holding onto the passenger bar, whilst my mind moved into an altered state. When you disconnect your brain to the point of near sleep, pain becomes so much harder to feel.

★ ★ ★

Twenty-four hours later, I had successfully collected the money with my temporarily produced passport and the group in close watch. I stroked the soft fabric of the notes in my hand and a sense of hope began to dwell, like a distant flame, beside the Western Union. Suddenly, Akim took the wad of notes and my most valued personal document.

'We look after this for you,' he said with a wry smile.

'He is like your father now, you see,' Hadar added.

Instead of reacting with any words or arguments, I simply wandered back with my captors, like a deeply-hypnotised subject with three master illusionists, resigned to my fate, dreaming of what might have been had I taken a different route a day earlier.

Earlier that day, Akim had made me use Facebook to 'friend' him and share the pictures taken at the crocodile park, showing a vague concept of friendship to anyone who saw them. However, being locked in the hotel room for four hours while they disappeared off was an indication of the false reality that I myself had to promote. With the absence of a working TV and no food or cigarettes to distract myself with, I started to force a fantasy belief that perhaps this was all good for me and that, actually, these guys liked me. Maybe they felt pity for me and wanted to harden me up? Perhaps they would eventually move on and leave me to go home, passport and cash in hand, toughened for the road ahead! These thoughts ran incoherently with the true reality that I was a poor excuse for a hostage and, when enough money came through, they would leave me dead and buried, with photographs on the web to show they had left me alive and happy, best of friends.

The men returned early that evening, a little drunken and clumsy, knocking into the furniture within the cramped room. I felt somewhat relieved that I wouldn't be sitting in silence any more, but also worried at the thought of what these guys were capable of once their inhibitions were removed. Hadar sat down next to me on the bed, the smell of alcohol and cigarettes heavy on him. He rolled back his shirt sleeve on his right arm while occasionally glancing at me to see if I was paying attention.

'You see this scar?' he said clumsily.

I nodded at him and looked on. The scar reached across from his hand to near his elbow, with two larger smudged scars in the middle. He lifted his hand in the air before making the hand sign for a gun.

'I was fighting with my brothers in war and I was shot. I was hit twice here in the arm, but managed to kill him after.'

As Hadar ran his finger down the scar, Akim and the Doctor sat themselves in front of us on cheap wooden chairs.

'We were in a war zone and had no help,' continued Akim, 'but the Doctor, he treated him. He took the bullets out and sewed up the wound.'

'No painkiller,' the Doctor said.

'What did it feel like?' I said, feeling very out of place in the conversation.

'Like lightning and cutting,' Hadar said through gritted teeth.

We sat for a minute in silence while the information was absorbed. No one broke the silence, or even moved.

'We decide that you come with us to the islands,' said Akim suddenly. 'You e-mail your father and tell him you need this much.' He leant forward, producing a scrap of paper with a figure.

I looked at the amount, which was almost ten times as much as before. I knew instantly that leaving with these guys to go somewhere even further from home was not on my list of things to do, but I didn't believe for one second that I had a say in the matter. With this money they could easily carry on touring around on a reasonable budget and, considering the routine they had me in now, I knew that I didn't factor into these costs.

I typed the e-mail quietly, sitting in an awkward position on the bed while the men busied around the room getting ready for the evening's events. I was so tired and lacking in imagination that I couldn't think of any way out; my face becoming stone-like and rigid, accepting my imprisonment. Behind locked doors, three storeys up in a fake hotel building and full of forced fatigue, I was giving up and enjoying what I could of the silence, lying on top of an unchanged bed with the lights on.

After getting a few hours restless sleep in the small, smelly room, I could hear footsteps coming up the stone steps and landing towards the room. The sound of raucous laughter made me feel sick, knowing that they were near and my peace was over. Hadar burst into the room extremely drunk, with what at first glance appeared to be a female prostitute, but after a few seconds' gaze I could see that this was a lady boy. An obvious lady boy at that, with a very male laugh and voice.

I slowly moved myself from the foetus position onto my back.

'You fuck her!' Hadar said while holding her arm.

'No, I can't. I don't want to,' I said sheepishly.

'You fuck her and prove you are man,' he said angrily.

'I'm tired and ill. I can't. I don't want to,' I kept moaning.

'What are you, a woman? You are pussycat,' he said aggressively.

I could feel my sadness and pride aching inside my head and the throb continued to grow, where normally tears would emanate and refresh me. The anger started to germinate from the sadness and rage filled inside me. I looked at him with a reddening face and dilating eyes, wanting to tear his flesh from his body and burst him into a bag of blood and meat.

'I can't stand this!' I roared at him, while crawling up into a standing position.

The lady boy looked terrified and backed out of the now unlocked door, while Hadar stood surprised and impotent as I got up and squared up to him. Something within me stopped me from attacking him, although my gaze and breath were within inches of his own. I stood for a few seconds in a face off, before letting my thoughts separate from my physicality and I moved out the door with speed towards the landing.

The other men were now all watching me pace up and down in small steps near the windows of the landing, spit frothing out my mouth as I chewed over pure hatred, vying for release. My elbow lashed out behind me in a sudden unprovoked action and struck the window pane, smashing it instantly. With the second it took to break, my anger seeped away and my thoughts normalised, giving wind to fear on its highest level yet.

'You maniac!' Hadar shouted.

He looked very angry and red-faced, the others simply watching in astonishment as the scene unfolded. I went down the stairs very fast and could feel the warning signs of danger following me, like a man possessed. Hadar was coming down the steps after me, bellowing inaudible sounds. I ran through the foot spa hallway and exited the glass doors onto the street, where I stopped and surveyed the scene around me, keeping a close eye on the door. I thought that if I was out on the street then I wouldn't have to worry so much. Surely he wouldn't kill me in the morning light outside a McDonalds!

'I kill you!' Hadar shouted as he walked through the doors.

He picked up a bottle from outside the doors and smashed the back end over a stone bench. He checked it over for the appropriate lethal edges and headed towards me like a man possessed. I kept my arms out wide, like most Englishmen are seen doing outside pubs and football riots, protesting innocence but provoking the person slightly with a brave open chest.

'You can't just kill me!' I said defiantly.

'I cut you dead,' he said with devil eyes.

I looked behind me quickly and then back to Hadar whilst stepping backwards slowly. I was going to have to make a run for it and find help. This was literally my last chance. On the count of three, I turned and ran barefoot up the street, continuing for a minute or so at full pace. I looked around and saw that he had gone inside or disappeared out of sight. Despite my painful feet and lack of any real possibility of being taken seriously by anyone due to my lack of documents and basic clothing, I looked around and took a deep breath of exhilaration.

I ran into a fairly smart-looking, upmarket hotel I had seen when I first arrived. I figured that if I could find an English-speaking employee I could do my very best sales pitch on them, explaining the situation simply: that my passport had been stolen, but I knew where it was. With everything against me, except my human survival instincts powering me through, I approached the manager of the hotel and explained my situation, using my school-taught posh voice and emphatic goal that I would pay him well for helping me. It appeared I had been extremely lucky in my timing here, as the manager on the shift was a Japanese gentleman who spoke perfect English.

'I will help you because I believe this is the right thing to do,' he said very politely.

The manager spoke to the police in Thai as I sat in the air-conditioned reception. I started to wheeze a little, anxious as to how this might pan out. Ultimately,

I just wanted my passport back and the manager to let me stay while I got myself sorted out. I needed to make sure the police understood this and, while I psyched myself up, I kept thinking of all the horror stories I had heard about the Thai police from the rat-faced boy and my captors.

Within a few minutes a policeman arrived on a motorbike and walked into the lobby and, to my surprise, he beckoned me over to outside the hotel doors. I looked nervously at the manager, but he raised his hands in goodwill, sensing my apprehension.

'He knows what to do,' he said calmly. 'I have told him everything. You go and get your passport.'

'Thank you,' I said gratefully.

I rode on the motorbike with the Thai policeman and pointed directions for him to follow as we drove to the relatively near destination of the foot spa hotel. As we lurched on the old-fashioned but powerful motorbike down the last stretch towards the building, I could see three figures, heavily-clad in equipment of some sort, walking out the glass doors. As we pulled up outside, it was clear that my captors were making some sort of early escape from their dwelling, with huge bags packed and strapped to them like an expedition team.

'I want my passport back,' I said as I climbed off the bike.

'You take it then,' Akim said as he drew out the document from his pocket.

The policeman, who obviously spoke very little English, stayed silent opposite the men, holding his helmet and staring with contempt. Perhaps he was disgusted at them, or perhaps he was just sick of dealing with stuff like this; either way, he hated the sight of them and his body language, combined with the loaded gun, was enough to make the three of them act very differently.

'He gets looked after by us. He has drink, food, fun,' Hadar said to the policeman.

Akim handed the document to the policeman, who quickly passed it to me in a beat. The whole time, he kept looking at the men and stayed silent, prompting a fearful look in the men's eyes. It was as if they were on a precipice of something very dangerous and close to falling in.

'You have no friends after this!' said Akim as he looked into my eyes with hatred. 'When you in England, you think you have friends, you will have none!'

That sentence rang into my head like an echo and I couldn't shake the strange conviction he had within his message. It seemed so strange that this man could know anything like this, or formulate such a guess, as a parting shot at me and his failed entrapment. For now, I would choose to bury this somewhere else; instead, I needed to concentrate on getting myself home, an objective I had come to believe was out of my reach.

The revealing e-mail messages which bounced between my father and me that morning showed that I was on the thinnest ground possible and he did not believe a single morsel of the story I had written. He had imagined that I was off to the islands and that I had begun a stable adventure with some new friends, giving him some much-needed peace back at home. The truth, however censored, was an unpleasant and implausible chunk of reality that he didn't want to digest and, in truth, I couldn't blame him. He did, however, send me some money and my return flight was organised, leaving me with one full day and night of rest for the first time in a long time.

I knew that I had reached an impasse with my family and that I was probably more alone now than I had ever been in my life, but I couldn't feel sorry for myself and dwell on it. I had to try and make something work. I felt like I had survived something and now I had a second chance, something that I clearly recognised and cherished.

As I lay on the cool clean sheets of my room, slightly dampened by the water dripping from my clean, revived body after a long hot shower, I closed my eyes and felt complete and utter joy at the simple, fantastic contentment of being safe and warm.

Escaping the impossible

In the eighteen century, psychics would use children in their parlour tricks to enhance the spooky atmosphere. The child psychic would wear manacles that would, in turn, be tied to the table to show they could not be responsible for any goings on in the room when the lights went out, such as tambourines shaking and tables bumping on the ground. The manacles themselves appeared rigid but, if you knew the puzzle, it was easy to unchain yourself quietly and make mayhem in the room. Like most terrible claustrophobic scenarios, the manacles are analogous to the psychological effect in that we, as human beings, will restrict ourselves in situations through fear. However, it is our transposing of these problems that enables us to unshackle the manacles and find a solution.

* * *

On the long flight home, I felt indifferent towards the luxury I suddenly found myself in. I sat dressed in the same jeans and trainers I had been wearing for weeks, while the new underwear and t-shirt I'd bought on the way to the airport were the only things that afforded me some semblance of normality. The time spent in the Foot Spa Hotel had enabled my arms to heal and a flicker of colour to return to my face, promoting ambiguity amongst the travellers heading home. I ordered a large scotch on ice before any food arrived and drank, almost as quickly as it had been put down. The alcohol hit me hard, having abstained for the last week.

I decided that I couldn't go home to my parents after all this and see them struggle in my presence, listening to the stories of a million troubled young men rolled into one. Instead, I decided to head for the only people I knew who still liked me and owed me a favour. The two men, who had been my friends for the past two years, were a gay couple living in South London and I had an inkling that, if I were lucky enough to catch them in time, during what was the early part of a Friday evening, I would find a temporary refuge. Only four months earlier, when the two of them had had an almighty row and one of them needed somewhere to live for a week, I had taken him across London at one in the morning to stay with me and a girl I was seeing. During that time, I had kept him fed and watered and entertained, allowing a little space and sanity to preside while they fixed their relationship.

Their names were Julian and Michael, and it was Michael whom I had aided with a place to stay. In the relationship, Julian was the breadwinner, domineering and intelligent, always at work come hell or high water. Michael was the talented computer programmer, who acted in complete submission and high velocity as the camp counterpart.

Michael was tall and thin with short brown hair, and a feminine sensibility that shone in all situations. He had been brought up in private school and talked with pride, often acting quite ferociously to any criticism. He had a smile like the Joker from Batman and, with a dry humour and impeccable acting qualities, he made people feel that he wasn't one to cross.

Julian, in contrast, was very straight-acting. He was short, at five foot eight, and athletically-toned from years of private school sports and regular gym work. He was loud and never shone away from displaying his northern accent and cultural roots, his jokes and masculinity always a sign of insecurity. His brown eyes were dark and impossible to read; sharp and focused on whoever was talking to him.

I had travelled with my newly-exchanged money to their South London flat in fairly quick time, worrying the whole time in case they wouldn't be in or had moved. It was a calculated risk that I needed to work and, due to the rain and penetrating cold, I was in deep fear of having to go home if it failed. When I buzzed on the intercom in the tinkling rain, holding myself with freezing arms, I was relieved to hear someone answer.

'Ollie, is that you?' came Julian's voice.

'Yeah, I'm back from Thailand,' I said.

'Come in mate,' he replied.

That night, after the surprise caused by me turning up straight from the airport and with barely anything to show in the way of luggage, we talked and laughed and I was treated to a shot of GBL to warm the cockles. It had been a long time in my mind since I had experienced the delights of a modern Western living space, with friendly faces and English TV in the background. *EastEnders* was churning away in the background and I allowed the GBL to convert in my body into something wonderfully anaesthetic and familiar.

★ ★ ★

During the hours that I slept on their sofa, I was left home alone so that they could continue a weekend odyssey in gay club land. I woke up only once to send an e-mail to my father explaining my plans, and a check on my social media sites for any relevant messages. Despite thinking that it would be a bare cupboard in my inbox, I was very surprised to see a heap of messages from Anthony who, ironically, was online and still frothing at the mouth to speak with me.

Anthony: You think you're clever arsehole but you're not!

Me: What do you mean? Are you referring to me getting home safely from that shithole?

Anthony: Getting home safely… You'll be in hospital at least when I get you cunt!

Me: You had something to do with all that shit out there?

The shitheap gangsters and thieves…

Anthony: Listen dickhead you've got a runaway mouth!

Me: Well fuck you. I'm home now and you should be a little more mature for your age. How long you've known me and still you could see me end up like that?

Anthony: You think you've got friends at home? You've got none!

Me: What's that supposed to mean?

Anthony: You work it out smart arse.

I ended the conversation, trying to work out why his words sounded so familiar. Was I starting to go insane? Was every little link, no matter how small, beginning to have more meaning?

The effect of the tiredness and stress of the sudden vicious conversation had created an effervescent bomb in my head, culminating in a need to smoke a cigarette and get my body in the upright position. On the table was a piece of paper folded upright, like a birthday card. Inside was a handwritten message:

'Call this number and help yourself to whatever you want. We are in the Triangle – Michael'.

The flat was modern and situated on the waterfront; the sound of lapping waves and gulls floating within earshot of the windows meant that the living room was fairly swank and cool by anyone's standards. The leather sofa I had been sleeping on faced out onto a large open-plan living room and dining area, where the wooden table and designer furniture, comprising of pastels and blacks, contrasted with the room efficiently. I looked out of the bay windows and saw the first lick of light was beating onto the Thames, cold and blue frost emanating against the pane.

I rang Michael on the number provided and he told me to get in a cab and come down to the Triangle Club area, where he would get me into some club. I felt excited and yearned for the joys of being a welcomed friend, aware that the euphoria from the trials and tribulations of the night would be lying in wait for me.

Without changing my clothes, due to the fact I had none, and collecting a spare key and pack of cigarettes for the journey, I headed off in a minicab towards the club. Sitting in the soft cheap material of the Mondeo, I felt the warmth of the heater blasting against my legs and watched the rain splat on the window shield in relative morning darkness. I said nothing to the cab driver the entire way, soaking up the London radio as it repeated hits, all of which sounded familiar and comforting when, normally, I would have hit the off button straight away.

When I met Michael outside the club, I could see that he was already very merry. The excesses of the night before were long since underway and revellers cheered and marched up and down the rainy street as if it was a summertime parade.

'We have to go to a friend's house across the way,' said Michael. 'I'll jump in.'

We pulled up outside a smart apartment building and headed into a glass foyer, where several lifts waited in anticipation of lifting us hundreds of feet in the air towards the penthouse home Michael was busy describing to me.

'Julian is already here. This is James's house and I have to sell him some bits,' he explained.

On his back was a large rucksack that looked filled to the brim. The odd combination of his designer clothes and this hiking bag hung over both shoulders made me feel ill at ease, knowing the probable quantities of drugs laden inside.

When the oak-framed front door opened we were greeted by a tall, pale man with sharply-defined facial features, wearing shorts and an open shirt. He was sweating profusely. His eyes were pale blue and pinned pupils scanned us from head to toe without as much as a quiver from his mouth.

'So this is your friend, Michael. Very nice!' James said in an Irish twang.

We followed James into the carpeted beige hallway and immediately saw a glimpse of a man and woman entwined on a chair just beyond the open living room door. Sensing us almost immediately, the couple stopped kissing and looked at us with what I could only describe as daggers as we walked into the front room. The area was filled with revellers and a light dance track was bouncing bass through the sound of high-pitched excitable chatter.

The couple comprised of a smartly-dressed, shaven-headed man and a young black woman wearing next to nothing, balanced perfectly on his lap, one arm draped around his shoulder and the other lifting a glass off the marble counter behind them. He seemed completely out of place in the room, very clearly straight and clothed in the fashion of a city boy out on the town as opposed to an all-weekend drug's dustbin. She appeared to be making an effort to be interested, but watched the room carefully rather than interacting. I could feel her eyes burning into the back of my head.

'Who are you then?' the shaven-headed man said.

'I'm called mind your own business,' I said in a cutting voice.

'Jesus! You kiss you mother with that mouth?' he said.

'Nah, I'm only joking, mate. I just don't like to tell everyone everything,' I replied.

I sat down on a chair beside them and Michael went out of the room with James, leaving me to my own devices. The shaven-headed man pulled out a wrap and a card and started shuffling drug dust out of the wrap onto a lamp table.

'You fancy a line?' he said.

'What is it?' I replied.

'Mephedrone.'

I looked at the tan powder. I knew that, given my experience of the drug, albeit very brief, it should have been white and, without question, the aroma should have been so strong, something akin to fertiliser, that it would have been making me wretch by now. None of these things were happening. In the interest of being open to new possibilities, and not wishing to offend a 'friend of a friend', I decided to try it. He handed me a note and I insufflated the powder quickly. Once again I noticed a flaw – the powder didn't burn. Given that I was also stone cold sober I should have been feeling the effects very quickly, but nothing was happening. My tiredness, together with the tediousness of the atmosphere, were growing worse. I smelt a rat, but I didn't know exactly what species I had discovered. If he was fooling people with this, it was because they were fucked-up on an alphabet soup of drugs; but I was sober and fresh out for the night (or, in this case, morning) and this meant I was a fly in the ointment for whatever plan he had.

'I've never seen mephedrone like that!' I said, whilst gazing around the room casually.

'It's new,' he said quickly.

'You want to do a shot of GBL?' I said.

'What's that?' he enquired.

"GBL produces another drug in the system called GHB; once that hits you, your brain floods with the lifeblood that keeps it happy and which scientists call Dopamine. It is similar to Ecstasy, but it is lethal and the slightest overdose is likely to kill you. It is important to time and mix the drug well with something stimulating, otherwise you're going to have a seriously bad time."

This was very strange that a man at a triangle after-party full of drugged-up people swigging GBL every hour on the hour was asking me what it was. I looked in his eyes, which were levelled and honest, not a bead of sweat or tiredness touching his otherwise perfect skin. He was either trying to catch me out or he was such as newbie at this scene that he knew nothing and, therefore, was a danger to himself and everyone around him. If he had just accidentally come across this scene through a girl and was innocently asking questions, then this was an unfortunate party at which to do it. A much more likely possibility, given the copious amounts of drugs around and semi-dangerous people, was that he was an undercover policeman. The looks and clothes were fitting of an uneducated young copper, and the plausibility that he was here because someone had been busted and agreed to bring him into the scene in exchange for leniency was becoming a strong possibility in my mind.

I heard the door open behind me and Michael leant down and tapped me on the shoulder.

'Can you come here, please, mister?' he said.

I followed him into the hallway, where a tweaked, frightened-looking version of my friend stood in front of me, breathing heavily.

'Have you just done something?' I said.

'Why are you talking to that guy?' he said quietly.

'I don't know. He was there and I started talking,' I replied flippantly.

'I think he's a copper. James might be in some trouble,' he whispered.

'Well, he did just offer me fake drugs and he seems like that.'

'Why were you talking to him, then?' Martin said angrily.

'Calm down,' I replied.

It was obvious that things had become complicated since I had been away; in fact, it may have become that way even before. The state of the gay scene had grown much more dangerous and drug-infested than the straight scene within the last five years. Police were heavily profiling the triangle area, as the clubs within it had previously been given a 'blind eye' approach, allowing clubbers to use drugs without fear of detection from bouncers or anything else. The method was used on the basis that it contained and controlled, limiting other problems and wasting resources, but the effects could be extremely varied. With any drug, no matter who uses it or whether it costs a lot of money, the end results can be lethal. This cause and effect was becoming more and more regular and the nights spent partying into the early hours had started to carry a stigma. I myself hadn't been clubbing for a while and my need to take drugs had retreated to a lonely home affair, just like tens of thousands of people falling into the same trap all over the world.

We gathered Julian from the bedroom and hastily made our way downstairs, saying goodbye indiscriminately to the people in the living room and avoiding any explanations to the party-goers. We stood by the main rood adjacent to the building and hailed a black cab, which we directed to take us back to base as soon as possible, a shaking Michael and slightly blank-looking Julian silently filling the leather seats at the back of the cab.

During the ride home, it transpired that Michael had lost his job recently and Julian was 'changing jobs', although this was not fully explained. This seemed to answer a question never asked about the drug dealing I had witness that evening, which was clearly a much larger enterprise than a one-off. I felt ambiguous about the subject and didn't see any reason to pry, instead asking point-blank if I could stay in their spare room and pay some rent. It would be sub-letting and that was potentially against the rules, but the timing seemed to be perfect and I needed somewhere to live. Their lives may have become slightly more chaotic, but they were fond of me and the lifestyle was interesting and lively, a point I deemed absolutely essential to living a happy life. My immaturity was only matched by the curious, unexplainable tension that filled theirs, the sunlit cab ride home cooking our psychic juices into a paranoid frenzy.

★ ★ ★

Having completed a transfer of rent and auxiliary cash to Julian, providing me with a month of living outside the family home courtesy of my father, the rode to a new life of London luxury was paved in front of me. Michael was frantic in the early morning light of day and scrabbled between the front room and the hallway on the home phone. I felt exhausted already from the night before, having avoided sleep and topping myself up on cigarettes and drugs, hoping for more excitement before concluding the day.

'I have to go to Ben's house. He wants me to look at something urgently,' Michael said through tensed pale lips.

'You have to go *now*?' I said quizzically.

'I'll be back by this evening,' he said impatiently while wheezing on a cigarette. 'Julian can keep you company till then.'

'I thought we could go over to a friend's house,' Julian said to me. 'They have crystal over there.'

I nodded along at the plans and sat back in the creased leather sofa, the piercing light from the window highlighting my dishevelled appearance. The adrenaline from my impromptu arrival had faded, with nothing more than the mephedrone keeping me functioning. Michael left shortly after the announcement and took his laptop and various electrical chargers, leaving Julian and me with nothing left to do but order our own cab to the mystery friend's house.

When we arrived at the central London address thirty minutes later, the streets were filled with weekend normality. Bars and restaurants were populated with multi-cultural persons, sipping tea or gulping beer between friendly conversations amongst their peers. The door to the flat was located next to a cab office along the busy street, and we stood waiting for a fuzzy reply from the intercom, while hundreds of people swam behind us on their way to normal activities.

I felt the eyes of the strangers cutting into my sweaty back, my paranoia exacerbated by the artificial chemical drive in my bloodstream. My sun-tanned face felt faded already and a sense of dread and loneliness replaced my rational thoughts. I could smell a strong minty chemical emanating from my skin, and I lifted my right hand to my nose and smelt my fingers to examine them further. With mephedrone, as well as some of the new legal highs, the molecular chemistry means that it is very water soluble and seems to leak, like butter through a sieve, into the outer layers of your skin.

We climbed a claustrophobic, dirty old staircase up three floors to reach the apartment. I could hear a baby crying somewhere within the building, the high-pitched notes jangling my brain into scrambled egg. What greeted us when the door opened was a strange and horrifying sight; a young, effeminate man twirling long, pointed ivory sticks, and an old toothless man dancing about with sweat streaking his bloated skin. As we moved inside and the music became louder, my heart began to match the fast repetitive beats.

★ ★ ★

Back in South London, inside Austin's swamped dirty flat, the crack-addled maniac of old, several undesirables filled the room sharing a stubby old pipe containing substandard drugs. A knock at the door moved Austin from his chair to the hallway, where he quickly used the viewing screen to monitor the person who was seeking entry.

'It's me,' said the voice behind the door.

Austin quickly opened the door and felt a flush of anxiety run through his body. It was a police officer, someone who used Austin as an informant. Austin was the kind of person who got into trouble often, mainly because he would pick up drugs several times a day, looking a state every time, and also because he had a big mouth that ran loose in all the wrong places. Austin was also of special interest to the police, having grassed on several dangerous elements over a large number of years and had committed crimes relating to the harassment of young women. He was a vile, mentally disturbed man who posed a threat to his friends and enemies, and even those that didn't know him.

He was a large, heavy-set man dressed in casual modern clothing and clean trainers. His appearance was completely normal by anyone's standards, ably demonstrated by the fact that he could blend in with any surroundings without being noticed – as long as we're talking about an average London street, that is. Years of working with the underworld meant that he had taken drugs infrequently and, of course, binged in order to fit in and sip information from the citizens around him. A mop of dark brown hair and sharp brown eyes fitted a large, weathered face, and the lines of time were fairly discreet. If he wasn't always playacting such a mentally-imbalanced drug-taker in group scenarios, then he would simply pass as a hard man. However, the slow, slightly high-pitched northern voice set everyone at ease in any room he occupied.

'Is he here?' said the man standing in front of the door.

'No, he's not. I heard he was back from Thailand, though,' said Austin, backing against the wall.

'Yeah, I know that. We don't have a mobile for him, no personal numbers to trace.'

'Well, I don't know what to say,' Austin replied sarcastically.

The officer looked around the hallway and then poked his head around the doorframe, looking inside the flat.

'Very soon you might be under investigation for harassing a minor,' the officer said casually. 'A fifteen-year-old girl. Not exactly an everyday occurrence for most middle-aged men! I've got a brand new file just waiting for a case, and a crack whore who needs some evidence to make her go away.'

'Look, you can't just fit me up for something like that,' Austin whimpered. 'You know I won't survive a charge like that, what with my history!'

'Scum like you don't deserve anything. I'll get what I want, when I want!' the officer barked. 'We've been down this road before, Austin.'

Austin paused before answering, his eyes displaying disgust and fear at the same time, while his mouth quivered.

'I told you, he sometimes hangs around with a dangerous lot and a heap of drugs – maybe he is right now,' said Austin. 'But he's not in contact.'

'Good! I like it when you tell me the truth.' The officer cleared his throat and, without warning, grabbed at Austin's shirt. 'If he does turn up, though, I want you to tell me straight away. You never know, the angel of mercy might just make an appearance.'

'I don't understand. If you know he's not here, then why do you care if he turns up later on?' Austin asked innocently.

The crackle of hoarse laughter trickled down towards them from the living room. Austin was impatient to get back to his drugs before they all disappeared and hoped the conversation would end soon. His was becoming increasingly annoyed at the fact that he was covering up for someone else, even if it was to get himself out of trouble, and he knew that he wasn't strong enough to be fighting dirty but powerful cops over bullshit charges.

'Look, I don't know anything yet, but I'll contact you if I do,' he said. 'You have to give me time.'

'Well, don't take too long, sweetheart. Think of your dear old mum and what she'll think if you get done for being a perv!' The officer leaned in. 'She's just survived cancer, hasn't she?' He paused and bit his knuckles in parody. 'Wouldn't want to upset the old bat, now, would we?'

Austin could feel the rage building inside him, and his quivering lip and shaking hands pulsated at the thought of striking the man in the face. The fear held him still in the grip of terrible stress, knowing that one wrong move would destroy what was left of his life. The officer smiled, revealing crooked teeth and yellow staining. Then he turned and walked away into the artificially-lit hallway.

* * *

Julian and I sat down on a small cushioned sofa, opposite the two freaks that had opened the door. We had all been handed Pyrex pipes of varying sizes by the toothless old man, with a sprinkling of crystal meth for each bowl. The flat was small but, in fairness to the effeminate host, quite stylish and clean. A lot of the cupboards and walls were adorned with either some sort of art or pashmina-style drapery, which gave a bohemian feel to the abode. I was fairly relaxed now that I was off the busy street and in a comfy seated position, despite the freaky people I had been introduced to. Given the recent experiences in Thailand, I decided to try and open my mind a little to what I was seeing and appreciate the friendliness that had been absent for many weeks of my life.

'We just need to stay here for a few hours and then we can go back and meet Michael,' whispered Julian.

'Why?' I said.

'Because there's some cleaning going on. You don't need to worry about it,' replied Julian before firing up his pipe and smoking a hefty flume of smoke.

The hideous old man sat, with folded legs, inhaling the drugs between wrinkled lips, while the lack of teeth showed a vacuum of space in his mouth. It was enough to make you feel ill. He wore an ill-fitting, white t-shirt under a purple, cross-patterned jacket made from some sort of wool, while his jeans and trainers denoted someone who was a lot younger. For some reason, his face seemed to be covered in an invisible evil that I couldn't explain –

maybe years of bad behaviour and twisted thoughts had mangled the subtle expressions.

'Here, why don't you try this pipe?' the old man said to me.

I took the extended home-made water pipe from the man and quickly examined it, feigning some sort of interest and mutual respect. I took my lighter and heated the contraption, filling it with thick smoke and inhaling slowly.

'That's it! Suck on the Devil's dick!' the old man said with joy in his tone.

I immediately stopped smoking the pipe; the revulsion of the comment and the fact it had come from such a hideous creature made me want to heave. However, I managed to hold it together and pass back the pipe, avoiding the gaze of the man.

Time continued this way for hours and hours, the darkness outside creeping through the windows, forcing lamps and ceiling lights on. I became extremely intoxicated with the strong substances being continually placed within me. I balanced the meth with GBL and used the drugs as if I was an imaginary apothecary, imagining scenes of old Frankenstein movies to juxtapose the sinister edge of the atmosphere in my mind.

I noticed that Julian was busy typing a message on his phone and I leant in, quite innocently, to see what he was writing. The message read *Start the night soon, money transferred, see soon*.

'What's that all about, mate?' I said to him.

'Nothing to worry about. There's a cab coming and we'll leave soon,' Julian replied.

'Fine,' I said happily, the previous query leaving my head.

'Look, I'm just going to nip to the loo,' Julian said.

As I watched him walk off through the living room door, I felt a slight unease at being alone with these strangers, even if it was only for a few minutes. The effeminate one was twirling his ivory stick again and looking directly at me, his gaze steely and unwavering.

'Would you like one of these?' The effeminate man held out a handful of blue pills towards me. I could see that his nails were extended and painted, his hands immaculate and long.

'What are they?' I said with interest.

'Well, we were on our way back from some club and just happened to leave these for another day. I can tell you, though – they will blow your mind!' he said convincingly.

'Well, I'm not sure. Maybe another time,' I said dismissively.

'Don't you trust me? Do you have a problem with me because I'm gay?' he said angrily, whilst recoiling back into his seating position, eyes narrowed and vengeful.

'No! It's nothing to do with that,' I said defensively, leaning forward in time with my now palpitating heart.

The effeminate man looked at the old man and they both started to smile and a relaxed demeanour fell over the room. I continued to sit up, straight and alert, but my heart and mind relaxed enough to take in the situation.

'Only joking, sweetheart! You have no need to worry. Any friend of Julian's is a friend of mine'. He spoke in a calming tone, resting his hand on my arm to reassure me.

I smiled and felt embarrassed for taking the original

action to heart, leaning back in the chair and taking comfort in the friendly camaraderie. For all the sinister pre-thought his joke had caused, I was now far more relaxed and I continued to smoke my pipe without much more than a cough breaking the silence. The only thing left, however, to cause a sense of unease in my mind was the twirling ivory stick in the effeminate man's right hand. His eyes were not following the twirl and it seemed alien to the rest of his body, carefully poised and controlled. I felt that maybe something on my part, by way of a friendly gesture, would ease the atmosphere that much more.

'Maybe I could try one,' I said through a forced smile.

The man handed me a selection of the pills and I picked one quickly, placing it straight in my mouth and crunching the bitter chemical. I never used water for pill-swallowing, finding that mastication of a drug was a quicker way of finding the high. The two strange men watched on as I chewed the last remaining fragments and smiled surreptitiously.

'Are you not having one?' I asked the men.

'Not right now, darling. Maybe later,' the effeminate man said.

'Fine, I suppose. I didn't want to be the only one, though,' I retorted.

'Where has your friend gone? It's been ten minutes since he left,' the old man said.

A shock suddenly shot through my body and I realised that it had indeed been a long time since Julian had gone out of the room. I got up off the sofa and headed towards the living room door, expecting the worse. When I opened the unlocked bathroom door, I found nothing, not even a light switched on. It dawned on me that he must have left the flat and obviously had failed to let me know. I didn't even know where I was or how to get back; all my money was in his possession, transferred to his back account given that my cards had been lost in Thailand. I walked back slowly into the living room to announce that Julian had, indeed, left me behind.

Without warning, a crashing, thundering roar of voices sailed up from the street outside and into the apartment; the three of us looked at each other in shock before adjourning to the window to view the action. Below, in the busy London street, a sea of men dressed mostly in black clothing and armed with batons were running two other men into the road and battering them with sickening blows. With the street lamps shining down on them, we could see the sticks bludgeoning their frail skulls and precious bones with the ferocity of bloodthirsty wolves. The two gay friends of Julian sat back quite quickly, leaving me perched over the ledge; I was trying to see why the police, who were mere feet away, were standing by their vehicles watching like frightened cattle.

'There's something in the air tonight!' the old man said.

'Heavy air. Violence in the darkness,' the effeminate friend said.

The doorbell rang and I leapt up from the sofa to answer the buzzer, with the two men watching with stern expressions.

'Come down, I have a cab,' said Julian through muffled tones.

I popped my head back round the door and said a

polite goodbye, hoping to escape from the flat and the area as quickly as possible. These two men were freaks and they had a nasty, sinister presence that rotted at my comfort zone. Despite years of education from my parents about accepting people for who they are and what they are, these two men were the epitome of when to say 'enough'. The conversations I had listened to had involved everything from gang rapes to stabbing wounds, major drug dealing to the punishments befitting traitors. The fact that they looked odd and had the human appeal of rotting rodent flesh was beside the point. In another life, not that far away in my past, I would have told these sick fucks what I liked when I liked, but the drugs made me weak.

'I wouldn't go back with them now,' said the old man.

'Why?' I said with a puzzled tone.

'It's not going to be good tonight. Something bad is going to happen,' he replied, evil lurking inside his wired eyes.

★ ★ ★

In the cab ride home, we sat in silence, the car stereo murmuring at a minimum volume. I sat in the back seat of the old people carrier, slouching down to look through the grainy window. I was on edge after listening to the crazy old man and having been left by my so-called friend in the company of strangers, something that we both chose not to discuss.

I could feel something washing over my vision and making small patterns out of everything around me, the sounds of the nightlife drowning into one continuous noise. Waves of anxiety followed by crashes of calm were running through me; I wasn't sure if it was the situation or the drugs that were causing the reaction. Julian seemed to be so still and silent, like a dead body propped up in the front seat.

Eventually, everything went black and I was neither asleep nor unconscious, just there in the moment with time ticking by without coordination. If you've ever listened to the streets during a rainy night while you're tucked up in a warm bed, you'll remember the sloshing rhythms of the rubber hitting dirty puddles and engines revving through tired gears. These were the only sounds left in my head until, eventually, even that tonal familiarity became distant and troublesome.

★ ★ ★

When my eyes opened, I realised I was being pushed inside the guest bedroom that was now technically my home. I was kneeling on the floor, holding onto the door with useless, clumsy hands, and I could see new faces and old faces standing in the hallway looking down at my powerless face.

'Help me, please?' I said drunkenly to Julian, who was holding my arm quite tightly.

'No!' was the sound that seemed to emanate from his mouth.

I don't know if I passed out, or the other people around me had simply left me alone and I was too messed-up to know, but I opened my eyes to a vacant hallway. I felt so weak and fragile, my mind spinning and whirling me to the left. I began to crawl towards the living room along the wooden floor, where I could hear muffled sounds of people talking. My heart was beating like a steam train and I didn't know if I was dying or tripping out; the answer was probably both. Time seemed to move faster and slower within blinks of the eye, my spiralling sense of balance causing me to spew tiny amounts of hot laver, like sick, out of my mouth.

When I reached the open living room door and tilted my head forwards, I saw something troubling. The effeminate man from the flat was sitting across from my dying form, legs crossed with a cigarette perched in his mouth. It seemed to take an age as the tall, sinister man got up and headed towards me.

'What is my name?' he said calmly, looking at me with eyes as wide and dilated as one could imagine.

I couldn't answer. Instead, I repeated my cry for help in whatever slurred, dribbling manner poured out.

'My name is Winston Black,' the man said, almost in a whisper. 'I want you to listen to what I am saying and repeat it back to me.'

'I can't!' I said helplessly.

Winston lifted my head and looked into my eyes with enormous intensity; his pupils looked as if they were about to bulge out. All at once, I felt the strike of the hand as it hit my face, while the wash of sound and image made it difficult to follow what was happening. I crawled over to a pair of legs by the sofa, hoping that an attempt for help with a new person might save my predicament, whatever that may be. The dream-like state of my thoughts and vision sent all logic away and, as I crawled towards Julian's legs, I imagined myself as no more than an infant.

Thoughts of cracking shells and gooey liquid dropped into my mind as the sounds of the room become further distant and strange. For a second I saw the face of Michael, stony and unsympathetic, staring coldly at my disintegrating form.

'No!' I hear, the word tumbling from above in loud demonic voices.

Normality and sober surroundings hit me for a few seconds as I turned to lie on my back, the world around me crumbling and a sense of death imposing heavily on my mind. My fight for life and aggression to maintain reality faded and simmered, replaced by an apathetic, nonsensical composure.

Winston leant over me again, and I could see his bulging, evil eyes staring at me. He barked something that I couldn't quite hear. The pupils were replaced by spinning green boxes that seemed to terrify the very core of my being. Spinning boxes of toxic waste were all I could make out, lasering into my brain as inaudible sounds filtered somewhere deep inside me. Somehow I knew that I was alive and that there was danger around me, but the chemicals and forced commands from the negative witch-like controller, towering above me, forced fear and submissive despair into my heart.

★ ★ ★

I awoke again, this time lying on the single bed within the guest bedroom. The lapping waves from the Thames are heavy in my ears and the cold night air penetrates through broken gaps in the windows. I feel paralysed and confused and I choose to listen to the sounds around me, for fear that I am asleep.

Looking to my left, I see a chair in the middle of the room, directly under the light. A noose has been made and laid out across the chair, the mere sight of which makes me feel sick.

I didn't put the chair there, but it's clearly where I see it, I thought to myself. *Is this my only way out? I can't do something like that. I won't give up on myself! Does someone want me dead, or did I put this here?*

The thoughts ran through me like tumbling water.

I heard a cough, harsh and sore, break through from the wall on my right and I listened further for sounds of talking. A repetitive loop of barely audible music seemed to filter through from my left and I wondered if people were deliberately teasing me, somehow knowing that I was awake in this cold, abandoned area. I didn't feel in control, while the air around me seemed useless and lifeless. As I thought about where I was and what I was doing in this place, a sound of drilling came from behind the door to the room, with the slamming of heavy objects hitting the surface of the white wooden frame. I was concerned now in case I was being sealed within the room and yet I didn't move. The fear of the world outside the room was enormous and I sat, motionless, beads of sweat appearing at my brow.

The same cough as before now repeated on my right and I listened immediately to my left for the irritating music to repeat at a low, muffled volume. The sounds seemed to be on a loop and yet, somewhere, another sound was coming through into my head. A voice, giving me instructions or orders, was penetrating into my consciousness. I couldn't be sure that this was the case, but I felt something needed to make sense, before I gave in to the darkness.

★ ★ ★

Cold blue light shone through the window and streamed into my room, providing a sense of closure from the never-ending night. I forced myself to move off the bed and investigate beyond the cell door in front of my bed. I could feel my will trying to break through as logic and reason defy the impossible things that have been happening to me, but the essence of the unknown was so strong that I pushed reason away.

As I moved, incredibly slowly, off the bed towards the white bedroom door, holding both logic and fear at bay, I noticed that the sounds had gone and I was in control of my physical form once again. Despite this being an incredible feat, I did not acknowledge the breakthrough, instead noticing the stiff, crumpled jeans and dirty, ill-fitting top that adorned my body.

I turned the golden handle at the door and slowly pulled back at the weak object that had seemed so menacing moments earlier, and the tall, sinister man named Winston stood firmly in front of me. I looked into his eyes, searching for the strange green boxes in his eyes that I remembered so clearly.

'Well, I have met a lot of people in my time, but you really take the biscuit!' he said.

'What's happening?' I said in return.

'How do I put this? You have died, my dear soul!'

I thought of the incomprehension in front of me and decided that logic should come out and play. I looked down at the floor, trying to think of a decent response, and then back into his eyes, which now seemed to be spinning green once again. Surely I couldn't have died and still be facing such similar surroundings as the ones that I'd left, the flat that was home to drug parties and wooden flooring? I could feel new words tumbling out of my mouth.

'What can I choose?' I said.

'Give up your soul and save another,' he replied. 'Go back and try again, or take your chances.'

It seemed so obvious that this was a trick and I was being taken for a fool in some sick game. At the same time, the majesty of the stranger made me believe that I was foolish to try anything but allow myself into the game. I turned around in a three-sixty degree and viewed each door from the hallway, noticing that each was shut. Winston stood on, silently.

'This can't be what's really going on,' I exclaimed in a shy, nervous tone.

Winston grew in stature and pushed his face with the dangling eyes into my vision.

'If you aren't ready and you're wasting my time, you can go back where you came from,' he said loudly.

I thought in circles and wanted to believe that this was a trick or a dream, something that I could laugh at and, in turn, make someone else laugh, and admit to the crap that was going on around me. I felt terrified, stuck in a trance;

the thought of going through with the 'game' seemed to be the only option in my current state of cowardice. *If I am dead,* I thought to myself, *and God only knows it could have happened a million times over with my record, then this is the devil and I need to follow his rules.* Being alone in a frightening place was one thing, but this was another type of fear, a confusion that made me believe these things were happening.

'I'll save a soul,' I said off-handedly.

At that point, Michael came out from the door to my right and coughed harshly. He looked frail and skinny, his eyes dull and irregular.

'Are you coming with me?' he asked.

The shock and confusion was becoming unbearable. If this was a game and they were playing me for a fool, then one of my best friends was in on it. Added to this, he was a damn good actor.

'No… I don't know,' I answered nervously.

With that, Michael returned to his room and I immediately tried to follow, hoping for some sense of sanity inside the new area. Michael shut the door quickly; I tried the handle in desperation, only to find that it was stiff, like concrete, and wouldn't budge an inch. The strength of the door frightened me some more; the unworldly stiffness of the usually weak timber door was unnerving. Again, I thought that this might be real and that I might be dead.

At that moment, I could hear faint voices in the room where Michael had returned and I listened to the ghostly argument.

'He'll get a thousand more years,' said the first voice.

'He didn't even offer to save his family,' said the second.

'Let's burst them open,' said a third voice, giggling.

The slicing sound of a blade hitting a thunderous volume of liquid came from the room. I imagined a machete hitting loved ones at great pace, the bags of meat and bones exploding harshly. The thought made me feel guilty and extremely distressed; I put my head in my hands, feeling the terror of my situation begin to swallow me up. Could I have really heard that noise and those words? Was I really dead?

'What happened in Thailand?' I said to Winston.

'You never left,' he replied glibly.

I shivered as cold sweat dripped down my back, like sheared ice. I could sense hot vomit trying to reach up from my stomach.

'The men who were with me, they treated me okay?' I said in a twisted attempt at reasoning.

'They didn't treat you well,' he smirked.

'What happened?' I said, horrific thoughts overwhelming me.

'Fish food,' the devil replied quietly.

I could sense a tiny fragment of compassion from the authoritative controller now. Winston was answering the questions that I was too terrified to even think about. I decided to go further on with the game, but play with some insight, some street-wise intuition of sorts. I was never a religious person and I was still hoping that this was an extremely awful game that would end, but the majesty of the surroundings and performance around me gave it some credibility.

'What if I want to go outside?' I asked.

'It will be very cold out there!' he replied.

It seemed such an odd thing to say and, despite the obvious warning that it was almost certainly cold outside in London, it was loaded with other connotations. I ventured for the door and I heard Winston sigh with disdain.

Walking out into the morning light, I felt an extreme vulnerability and something about it seemed terrifying. I looked from the second-storey stairwell onto the street below and saw two joggers dressed in grey tracksuits, the sight of which seemed to dispel slightly the idea that this was all bullshit. As I continued to gaze on, the two figures turned suddenly and looked directly at me, their faces contorted and sharp, like blood-thirsty animals. I juddered backwards, hardly believing what I was seeing, and felt my mind twitch, as if it was electric. The joggers snarled at me and projected fangs.

I ventured carefully down towards the street, feeling like hunted prey, my heart beating uncontrollably. The corner shop, which was directly opposite the flats, was a milestone I desperately wanted to reach. When I got inside the shop, I moved like a sloth towards the counter and, with great courage, I looked up at the shopkeeper. Unlike the joggers, he was dressed normally.

'What can I do for you?' asked the shopkeeper.

I tried to speak but nothing came out. Now, after all the effort of getting here, through treacherous surroundings, I couldn't speak. I felt numb and bound, my lips sewn together. I walked out of the shop, embarrassed and terrified of what was happening. If the outside world was out of control, and I had lost the power of my own communication, then perhaps I should accept my fate. I walked across the road and buzzed the intercom.

'Can I come back?' I said humbly.

'Ah, it's a lost soul outside!' was the muffled reply.

I came back to the flat with my tail between my legs, ready to accept whatever was destined for me. My mind now seemed able to accept the unreality of the world around me. As I entered the flat, I discovered the person who had greeted me was Michael. The sight of him made me happy and less reluctant to wallow in the desperation of my situation, and I followed him silently into the now unlocked living room. Winston stood at the back of the room, already in sight as I followed my friend inside.

'You have returned!' Winston said dramatically.

With that, I fell into a dark slumber and felt my body falling as I tried to make sense of what was going on. With the slowing of the images and slight coordination returning, I imagined that I was in a dark maze with my friends Michael and Julian. I felt safe and calmer, in the knowledge that I was no better or worse than my human accompaniment. It was a time without words and no particular meaning, but the safety and knowledge that we were together and I was no longer alone meant an enormity to me. The sound of a murmuring voice seemed to reach from the walls of the maze. No matter how hard I tried, I couldn't quite make out the words.

When I woke, almost without warning, I was lying back in the bed of my guest room with Winston holding me by the wrist. I was weak and apathetic, concerned only with why he was holding two fingers on my wrist, as if connecting to me like some sort of electrical component.

'We are going to play a game,' Winston said.

At that moment I heard a faint voice calling from outside the room.

'We've been drilling him all night,' said the voice.

I looked at Winston's face and saw rising anger. The cause and effect of the voice and his reaction gave me a sudden hope that this situation was not quite what it seemed. Winston stared at me with bulging eyes; I saw the green squares that had so terrified me reappear and push my courage back into the depths of nowhere.

'I will tell you a word and it will be the code,' he said. 'Another person will be the killer and another will be the accomplice.'

I nodded, still in utter confusion, and Winton pointed to a magazine lying on top of the dishevelled duvet. Without questioning, I picked up the magazine and saw immediately that it was a free gay publication and a paragraph had been circled and left open for me to read.

'*Police have released CCTV footage of a vicious homophobic attack on two men in Charing Cross, London. A police spokesman said: 'The incident was completely unprovoked and the victims were lucky to escape with the injuries they sustained, as the violent nature of the attack could easily have resulted in more serious injuries.'*

As I read each word, I became hot and flustered, the anxiety of a pseudo Catholic guilt sweeping over me as if I was ten years old. I knew that I was a multicultural and loving person, but the feeling of isolation and hate that had begun to infiltrate my life made me wonder what I was being pushed into thinking. I could feel my lips tightening and the stinging, itchy burn of poison leak from my armpits and feet. Perhaps, if my world had become so difficult to understand and unreality was everywhere, maybe I *was* capable of doing something like this? Maybe I *should* be hated and vilified?

Winston got up and left the room, closing the door behind him. As the door shut, I felt my heart jump as the electric adrenaline yanked me back into the fearful situation. I could hear shouting and breaking glass, the sounds of which reminded me of violence on drunken nights out. Perhaps the familiarity of those sounds proved what a monster I may actually be! I wanted to cry and be left alone with my newly-found artificial guilt, but my fear of what was going to happen to me kept me locked down on the bed.

The door slammed open and all three of the men I had previously believed to be my friends stormed the room with hatred in their eyes. I looked to Michael, who was stony-eyed and unresponsive, while the other two circled the bed. I wanted to scream out that I had nothing to do with the article in the newspaper. The guilt and confusion caused me to stop, with the single thought that even admitting to understanding what their anger was about could indicate me as the perpetrator. I just wanted it all to end and to go to sleep; nothing could have been better than for the nightmare to end.

'I want to sleep,' I said, my vocabulary failing me.

'You'll sleep now,' said Michael.

With that, he plunged a closed fist into my side like a knife, emphasising pleasure in his face as he twisted and pulled back from the wound. I fell instantly asleep and back into the maze world that I remembered, from what seemed like mere moments ago. All the guilt and worry faded and my friends, Michael and Julian, were there helping me navigate, like happy children in an unusual fantastical world. I let go of the horror and counted back to the events when I first entered this dream world, moving up from the tormenting, terrifying starting level. Perhaps the games I played as a child, involving levels and achievements, somehow made this imaginary fortress more relevant, but I was now beginning to think that causality was non-existent. If I hurt someone or myself, took anything too seriously or negatively, then I was not taking advantage of the world I now inhabited. My fear had become frivolity, the passion for fun and games returned. However, I could sense a voice continually murmuring in the background; a low, inaudible chatter.

When I awoke again on my bed, in the now darkened guest room, I could see Winston's hand holding my wrist. Two fingers were placed over a certain crevice, as if checking my pulse, a thought that hadn't occurred to me last time. When he lifted his hand away, I thought I could see a string running from my wrist to his fingers, like a cable, but I dismissed the idea immediately.

'I am going to ask you to tell me what the answers are now!' he said.

'Okay!' I replied.

Behind me I saw a blue light shining and I turned to

see a shadowy figure nestled in the doorway to the room. Despite the dreamy, watery feeling of my surroundings, I could tell the light was coming from a mobile phone or a camera, and it was shining on me. For some reason, this didn't bother as much as the click of Winston's fingers, which brought me to his full attention as we now sat opposite each other on the narrow bed.

'Repeat back to me what the answers are when I say!' Winston said.

He mouthed the words and sounded out certain parts of the enunciation, the kind of action a child would use at school to covertly tell another of a secret. I looked carefully at his mouth and tried to guess the word, feeling almost enslaved and grateful for whatever ridiculous scenario I had been dragged into. Feelings of suicide, guilt, anger and isolation of such extreme forms had made me look at the devilish commander as some sort of helper. I wanted to please him somehow in order to be rewarded with more sanity.

I repeated the correct words and Winston pulled tightly on my arm, thanking me for the exercise. I felt a rush of drowsiness run over me and I could feel myself smiling and relaxing. I slept then, in darkness, the irritation of dreams gone. As I rested, the cold night, that had reached me so quickly during the horrors of my torment, dissipated into day.

★ ★ ★

As I lay on the bed, feeling sober but weak, I recounted times in my life when I had felt physical pain. I couldn't stop obsessing about the pain of memories and the actual pain that I had felt at that time. The world seemed normal again from the moment I had opened my eyes, but I was busy obsessing and making myself more comfortable on the sweat-encrusted sheets. The memories of the weird goings-on of the previous day were making me link in to terrible hits of emotional pain from times gone by. I had an urge to look in a mirror, wash my face or clean my teeth; instead, I sat staring at the ceiling, imagining some of the worst points of my life. In many ways, it distracted me from the embarrassment of what had occurred the previous day, knowing that, at some point, I would have to confront the people that I now saw as potential enemies.

Had I simply gone mad? I wondered. *Was there any comfort or conclusion that I could muster from this?*

Looking at the clock at the side of the bed, I realised it was only seven o'clock in the morning. I therefore decided to go back to my haunting memories before attempting anything physical.

PAINFUL MEMORY: RUSSIA, MOSCOW – 6 JULY 2005

My girlfriend and I had moved to Moscow at the beginning of summer to find a new life. I had been offered a new job there. I had worked in the city of London previously and, from a fairly young age, I took a good salary and wore a suit and tie every day.

The company I worked for had three umbrella

companies attached to it and the environment in their offices was no less alarming than swimming with sharks. On the first day at work in the Moscow office, I had created enemies and allowed myself to be ridiculed by suggesting that acts of terrorism should be insured against for individuals working in high alert areas, and the ensuing fallout meant that I kept my opinions to myself from then on.

My mentor took me to lunch in the afternoon on 6 July, to enable me to get a personal take on the city and feel more at home. I have to say that, because of the hostility that encompasses Moscow, getting used to it and feeling at home are two things that just don't happen. When we arrived at the small bistro-type place, we ordered a dish that comprised mash potatoes, sausage and salad. Not similar in style to the English bangers and mash, but more the German version of the plate.

At around 6.40 pm I began to feel ill and nauseas, my skin colour draining from my face and only bed becoming a sensible option. At around 10 pm I ran to the bathroom and vomited; I felt a burning pain run through my body, like miniature knives cutting fragile skin. The regularity of the vomiting increased over a half hour period, until my worried girlfriend saw blood entering the toilet bowl.

My girlfriend tried to get help from the neighbours, but nobody would even open their door. At this point, I was crawling out of the apartment. I knew that this was poison running through my veins, the pain being like nothing I had ever experienced before or after. When my girlfriend saw me convulsing by the door, she took my mobile phone and called the number last dialled, which happened to be my mentor. He then arranged a private ambulance to take me to a private hospital and I was treated within the next hour.

The doctor came to me at about 2 am when I was lucid and calm, pumped full of antibiotics and painkillers. He asked me straight if I knew what had happened, or if anything strange had occurred during the day leading up to the illness. I told him I simply couldn't remember. He alluded to the fact that I could have been poisoned based on the blood tests, because the normal counts for food poisoning as a norm were simply not there. He did say, however, that nothing was conclusive and, as I lay there with drips and entered into a new calm, I chose not to think about it anymore.

The next day, the terrible event of the 7 July bombings in London was shown on the international news channel. As I lay, in quite terrible pain, on a small, hard sofa near the television, I couldn't help but think that I could have been killed in one of those explosions given the time and place they occurred.

At that moment a very ill, weak-willed part of me wished that, maybe, I had. It was impossible to deny the thought had occurred; yet the repellent, illogical nature of it made me feel worse than I already did.

★ ★ ★

I got up from the bed and walked over to the mirror, which was balanced against the wall opposite the bed. The morning light was just strong enough for me to make out that my complexion and eyes were as dull as dishwater, with black arching crevices beginning to appear under my eyes where the apparent lack of sleep was beginning to take its toll. I opened the flimsy plywood wardrobe and took a view of what clothes I could borrow before venturing out of the room, picking up a pair of jeans and a black shirt that just about hid the disgrace that had appeared in the mirror only moments before.

When I walked into the living room, I found Michael and Julian both sitting on the sofa watching early daytime TV. Michael was wearing a grey towel-like dressing gown, while Julian had already smartened up in a black suit and white shirt. The room had the smell of coffee and toast, the sound of the show 'Frasier' covering the impending silence around us. The normality was comforting, but the headache I felt pounding away and the ache in my legs and back was one that I compared with an early memory of post-surgery.

'I borrowed these clothes. I hope you don't mind?' I said openly to the room.

'No problem, mate,' said Julian, reaching to his cup for another sip of coffee.

It appeared to be just a normal Monday morning, and the shame of my memories from the last twenty-four hours seemed almost too stupid and puerile to vocalise. I stood in the room without moving for a minute or so, feeling my heart beating with frustration at the confusion in my head. I looked down at the floor like a dutiful brow-beaten dog and pondered on my next move, wondering if I was already being considered the 'embarrassing friend you can't take anywhere'.

I surveyed my borrowed clothes in paranoia, checking that nothing embarrassing was sticking out or looking odd, testing my own sense of sanity and pride. I looked on at Julian in his suit, feeling jealous and embarrassed, thinking how smart I used to look on a Monday morning before my life became a mess. He must have sensed the stare, because he turned his face slowly in my direction and nodded, as if asking me to commence my question.

'What happened yesterday? Or last night, or whatever?' I bumbled.

'Oh, not now! Not again! We've been nursing you all weekend while you've been freaking out having nightmares and delusions,' he retorted angrily.

'What? You mean I was having nightmares?' I said pathetically.

'You have *been* a nightmare. You just can't handle your drugs,' Michael said without missing a beat.

'But Winston, the guy who was controlling...' I started.

'Winston is a very good friend of ours and he tried to help as well,' Michael cut in.

'I thought he was the...' I continued.

'Oh look, we have all agreed as a house rule that we are not talking about this, ever again,' Julian said, finishing his coffee.

I stood still, like a frightened child, my left arm cradled in my right, my legs almost buckling from the lack of strength and frailty. My stomach and arms looked much thinner than they had the last time I had checked. The jeans were almost falling down around me and the shirt was drowning me in material. I felt so weak and incapable.

'I'm going to have a wash and then try and sort out getting back across London for some work!' I said positively, forcing a smile.

The room lay silent and they both continued to watch the TV, my presence almost fraying the edges of any comfort. I walked back out of the room and headed for the shower, the dull ache in my thighs and sharp pains in my still blistered feet harrowing my sense of normality. Just like post-surgery, it was hard even to walk like a normal person.

* * *

Back in Ginoh, Thailand, the sun was beating down on the patio deck that surrounded the luxury apartment Anthony inhabited. He was sauntering outside the patio doors, wearing a silk dressing gown and sandals that made him look every bit the ex-pat gangster that he was. He was used to the temperature now and, even with the scorching sun frazzling his balding head, he strolled out into the full beam of the light smoking a liquorice roll-up. He pulled out his mobile phone and hit a memory button, pressing the slightly old handset to his ear.

'Your down payment is there, but I want to see further results quick march,' he said quietly into the receiver.

'You've seen the pictures, he was drilled all night! We'll finish off the rest in the next few days,' the voice on the other end replied.

'You need to get all the transfer details and rinse that cash pronto. If anyone figures out that it was linked to me or you, then this is going to go very wrong,' Anthony continued.

'Did you see the mess he was in? That must have been worth a laugh, right? If he tries anything smart, we'll get him fucking sectioned,' the voice said.

'Yeah, the cunt got was coming to him. But I want the money now!' Anthony whined.

'We've got him under control and the house is rigged up. We'll get the stuff we need from his family business and from him, to rinse the lot. But you got to know that we are taking our cut and I don't want any funny business,' the voice warned.

'Got it!' Anthony hissed out.

As he clicked the small handset off and placed it back into his flimsy silk gown, he stared out into the distance with a wry smile. The adrenaline and satisfaction gave him an almost sexual buzz and he bowled back into the living room, feeling twice the size he really was.

★ ★ ★

I returned from the shower into my bedroom, feeling slightly refreshed but still very frail. The mass confusion of what had happened and the fact that my friends refused to cooperate in helping me was making me feel as mad as a hatter. I couldn't argue with them because there was a strong chance that I had caused a scene and imagined stuff, or simply gone so crazy from the drugs that I didn't know what was going on. I did know, however, in my heart of hearts, that something occurred that was not under my control and I felt uneasy about accepting and trusting my friends. The conflict was huge and fearful for me, as these friends were now the only ones I had left to socialise with and actually count as mates. The sense of impending depression and lack of self-worth was highlighted by the dishevelled, bearded face that greeted me in the mirror as I picked up the used towel from the floor.

I head back into the living room, only to find Michael still sitting there, as Julian had left while I was in the shower. His laptop was open in front of him on the table, but he was busy vegging out watching the TV.

'Can I use the computer to check my e-mails?' I asked.

Michael gestured with his hand for me to help myself; he curled his feet underneath him on the sofa to make room for me to sit down. I logged on to my e-mail and set myself the task of getting in touch with my family, sorting out some cash and accessing work e-mails. The progress of making a few basic tasks seemed to be the best thing I could do for myself, and I sat perched on the edge of the sofa, attempting to look a little stronger than I felt in front of Michael. The system on his computer was loaded with huge arrays of programs and I knew, from my moderate knowledge of software and laptops, that this was a heavy duty machine.

A mere ten minutes later and I had achieved my tasks, announcing to Michael that I had finished, like a child to his mother. I felt desperate for approval and to eke out some sense of pride that I felt and knew I deserved, the weight and caustic nature of the guilt causing resentment within myself.

'That's good, mate. So you should!' was the only response I got.

A suitcase full of clothes was confirmed as being sent to the address and cash was transferred to my account, the communications of these tasks all having replied electronically. The probability of someone within my family wanting to verbally talk with me was far from realistic as this stage and I knew I had to sort my life out before bothering them again. The hollow prospect of receiving clothes and money seemed almost a last ditch attempt at salvaging some respect amongst these peers, and a cold throbbing pit of denial burst it stitches, leaving me clucking for self-medication once again.

I walked into the kitchen, casually glancing to my right at Michael, checking for any sign of awareness. I pushed on scanning for left-over drugs. The kitchen was small and windowless, filled with modern, lazy-man technology and designer fridge freezer. The black and white square-patterned lino floor was the cheapest part of the whole flat, stained with small amounts of food and indiscriminate powders. Michael had once shown me an evil streak by admitting to placing small amounts of caustic soda on the floor so that it mixes with any discarded drugs; if someone then decided to cluck around looking for substances, the resulting injury to their nose or lungs could be horrendous. I knew, therefore, that the only places worth looking would be above waist height.

I opened a small cupboard I knew had been used for hiding stuff in the past and found a small teacup filled with neat GBL and a small measurer. With a squeeze and drop of stale fruit juice from the side, I downed the substance and returned to my thin-walled room for some downtime.

★ ★ ★

Julian, dressed in a smart, single-breasted suit, crossed a busy main road in East London, feeling in his right inside trouser pocket for his razor-thin phone. The grey post-1980s architecture loomed overhead like overgrown moss and the chatter of Eastern Europe bounced across the roads from all directions. The freezing cold temperature caused Julian to pull his coat together momentarily as he flipped through a stream of numbers. Walking into a smaller private street, Julian entered a private members sauna.

'Let me in, quickly,' he said to the receptionist.

* * *

As I lay on the bed, feeling more and more relaxed with intoxication, I can hear the sound of the TV blaring from the other room. I'm feeling normal and sober, yet better and bouncier from the almost immediate relapse into chemical land. In this instance, I forgave myself more than I cared to remember for the need to be anaesthetised.

'Coming up this morning…' the faded sounds of the TV stopped suddenly.

I could trace light footsteps sauntering from the living room to the hallway and then into the next-door bedroom.

'I don't know, baby. I'm tired,' a muffled voice explained from the bedroom. 'Okay, I'll come, but I need to get dressed and put the stuff on.'

I knew that Michael was acting far more aloof than he ever had with me. He was ever the weaker side of the relationship and someone that, although it's something I have never done, I could easily bully. I listened to him walk into the hallway towards the main communal bathroom of the house, at which point I seized my chance to question him. I stomped off the bed and, with vigour, I pulled open the flimsy bedroom door and squared up to my frail-looking friend.

'Tell me what the fuck is going on, Michael!' I barked.

'Nothing baby,' he mews.

'Don't call me baby! Tell me what is happening.'

'Nothing, Mr Paranoid,' he replied, while trying to slip off into the living room. I followed him in.

'Look, I'm sober and strong enough to know the difference,' I shouted as he sat down, cross-legged, on the sofa. 'I am not accepting that bullshit I've been fed.'

Michael opened his laptop and started fiddling around, avoiding eye contact with me. He grabbed a lonely cigarette on the table and sparked up.

'You're roaring around here like a wild animal and behaving very badly,' he said.

'Don't try all that. You've got money for my stay and I am asking a question. Don't you care about the fact that I am your friend and I've helped you as a friend?' I asked in a hurt tone.

He looked at me in the eye for the first time and took a puff on his cigarette, holding my gaze for thirty seconds in total silence.

'It's not like you've been that nice, is it?' he replied. 'I came with you when you rescued me to that person's house and all the scary people kept popping in. Not exactly my kind of people.' He turned away from me.

'What about the people? Your boyfriend was beating you up! I come from a world where some of those so-called scary people would not have understood at all what it means to be different, but I was the one who stood up to them in the background and made everyone treat you like a prince, using every bit of my popularity and favours to help you.' I paused to take a breath. 'My own parents weren't even speaking to me and I had much more important stuff to do, but I put your needs ahead of mine because that's what friends do!'

He pulled a sullen face and shook his head, smoking the cigarette violently. Without warning, he picked up the laptop and mobile phone and stood up to storm past me. I remained motionless, trying to figure out what was going on. It was obvious something was happening because of the way Michael was evading my questions, but I was nowhere near finding out and was more frustrated than when I had started. Michael was now in his bedroom sulking and I was dreading what would happen next.

★ ★ ★

In the sauna, Julian walked into a small cubicle set off from the side of the facilities. It was a dank, desolate area, painted completely in black and featuring the cheapest type of materials known to the modern world. A CCTV image was being shown on a small screen eight foot in the air, just by the side of the cubicle, giving a four-way view of whoever was in the local vicinity. Inside the cubicle was a familiar figure, wearing a long waist towel and smoking a pyrex pipe.

'Winston, is the money there?' asked Julian.

'Yeah, it's there, but I need the passwords, codes and whatever else to do the money transfer,' Winston replied, whilst coughing through cold, blue, drug smoke.

Julian handed him a USB stick and took the pipe out of his hand.

'That Anthony sure is a guy with energy,' Winston said with amazement. 'He's tracked down and took a poker-faced stab at all his friends he thinks can be blackmailed and won.'

'Yeah, well...' Julian mumbled.

Just then, Julian's phone rang and he grabbed it out of the small travel bag he'd brought into the sauna. He snapped it open and listened with a blank face. Slowly, as the voice continued, his face dropped until it became menacing.

'He's going to find out,' he said down the phone. 'The computer is still full of videos of him and what we did, raw and all over the fucking place.'

Then he closed the phone and looked at Winston.

'We need to get back to the flat!'

★ ★ ★

The living room was in total silence. I had been sitting there now for an hour, TV off, radio off and blinds drawn. I could feel the rage within me, ready to do some damage. The bedroom door opened and I could hear Michael heading to the bathroom again, obviously wishing to avoid me and any further confrontation. I got up from the dining table chair and stomped after him, swinging the living room door open like a maniac. I could see Michael freeze by the front door, which had been double-locked and bolted by a key I did not possess.

'You have got to tell me what's happening before it's

too late. You said yourself you didn't like the people I know, and you also know that I will never truly let this go!' I spoke through gritted teeth, staring into the dilated pupils of my victim.

'What do you want from me?' he said humbly, tears welling up in his eyes. 'Do you want me to end up at the bottom of the barrel? Hit rock bottom?'

I heard the lock move in the door from the other side and the shuffling of feet. My heart jumped in my rib cage and I move backwards, away from Michael. My gut instinct told me something bad was waiting for me on the other side of the door. I walked slowly back into the living room, suddenly feeling unusually weak at the thought of what awaited me. I looked at the clock on the wall and saw that it was still only mid-afternoon. It was too early for Julian to be back from work.

Julian, Winston, and a third man, older and more intimidating, stepped into the living room like a pack and sat down on the seats and sofas without saying a word. Michael followed into the room slowly, hanging back by the door. I noticed, for the first time, that Michael was wearing odd shoes, with odd socks and short-legged dungarees, making him look completely insane. I was sure he had not been wearing these clothes earlier, and I began to feel very insecure.

'So what the fuck is going on?' Julian said.

'Well, look Julian,' I began, 'I know something is going on. If you guys won't tell me, then I want to call in the police and they can decide.'

'We are not calling the fucking police!' he shouts.

'You must have something,' I exclaimed. 'You said that

something was happening,' I said, looking at Michael for support.

Julian stood up ferociously, knocking over the chair and grabbing an empty beer bottle from the table. Without missing a beat, he smashed the bottle over the table, creating a weapon in his hand.

'If you want to know what really hard is, then just try it!' he shouted, his eyes narrowing. 'No wonder you've no friends left.'

I felt myself starting to sink into weakness and insanity again. I fell back into a chair, holding my hands snugly over my face to block out the world. I tried to make a next move, but my mind was gridlocked and all I could feel was exhaustion and pain. The world around me seemed hostile and impossible to navigate. The words he used I had heard before from someone, someone equally as hateful.

The memory of the chair in my room with a noose from the previous night jumped into my head and I immediately felt sorrow and anguish. I could feel tears gushing through the cracks of my hands and falling onto the varnished floor, the only sounds to be heard in the room full of people. The shame spread through my body like butter.

'You can't even dress yourself properly!' Michael said.

Opening my tear-stained hands, I looked at Michael standing in front of me wearing the odd clothes, and my brain seized-up. I couldn't think anymore and the confusion was too much to bear.

'Okay, can I order a cab?' I said with finality, looking at Julian.

'Yes, that would be best!' he replied as he sat back

down, a wry smile appearing on his angled face. 'Winston, go and collect his luggage.'

Winston stood up with an equally malicious grin and headed off to my room. He seemed unequivocally pleased with himself, and his wry smile gave him the appearance of a narcissist. I could feel my hatred for him bubbling like lava, the vile poisons damaging my insides.

Julian began tapping into his laptop, flipping through pages of porn with a vacant look on his face, a picture of calm and concentration following my public breakdown. It appeared as if he mimicked emotions by choice, not by catalyst and I wondered how I could be so blind when it came to choosing my friends all these addled years.

★ ★ ★

I arrived back in my home town and directed the taxi towards Austin's house, feeling unable to even contemplate facing my family or asking for help, as they would know that I would want drugs. Despite my family's clean-living, respectable way of life, we had enough connections to make problems go away; yet I was ashamed and confused about the prospect of receiving any help.

The atmosphere in Austin's house always made me feel better; I would compare myself to the desolate people that lingered there, providing a cheap source of confidence for me.

I paid the driver and headed upstairs with my small travel case, towards the familiar apartment; the smell and claustrophobic stairwell brought about an almost homely nostalgia. The door opened and a very surprised Austin stood leaning drunkenly around the frame.

'Well well well. What you doing here!' he said in his muffled London accent.

'I'm beaten up and in need of some help,' I said, pulling my case inside as I strolled past him without invitation.

When I stepped into the living room, I immediately saw Ben and recognised the smoke-filled living room as a refuge from the past, different and safer. The scenes in which I had been living made this place feel like a haven. I sat down on a chair and pulled my shoes off painfully, the blisters and redness on my feet having returned in full form. I winced as I took each shoe off and, for a moment, I considered the smell but carried on regardless anyway to alleviate the pain.

'So, what's happening?' said a wide-eyed Austin.

'I've been dipped and dipped out,' I replied.

'What, about Thailand?'

'I'm off the dragon, but I'm not in generally good shape,' I murmured.

'Good to see you, man,' said Ben, leaning over the arm of the sofa to bump his fist on mine.

I sit in silence for thirty seconds and looked listlessly at the floor, allowing Austin to take a seat in front of me.

'So, what's happened?' Austin asked. 'I know you've been back.'

'How?' I said without looking up.

'You know, people…' he replied.

'Do you remember the two gay guys you met last year?' I said, scanning the room.

'Yeah. The ones who got blood up my wall trying to bang up that meth shit!' he replied viciously.

'Well, they aren't my friends from the looks of it. They took advantage of me when I was weak after a load of shit from Thailand and now I don't know what's coming!'

'Well, I told you not to trust a couple of benders like that, but you wouldn't listen,' Austin spat out.

'I got kidnapped in Thailand and I think they had something to do with it. Well, at least after, anyway,' I said. 'I think money changed hands somewhere and I left myself open.'

'How did you manage to go to Thailand to get healthy and end up kidnapped?' Ben piped up.

'Because I made a mistake!' I snapped back. 'I am healthy and better off, but there's a lot of me to fix.'

We sat in silence, none of us looking at each other while contemplating the moody atmosphere of the room. Eventually, Austin stood up and walked towards a wall cupboard, pulling out a bottle of scotch. As he creaked back down into the chair opposite me, he poured a drink and sighed with a hiss of relief.

'What kind of problem are we talking?' Ben asks.

'I think they want some of the family money and they're going to blackmail me,' I replied.

'Think? How do you know they're going to blackmail you?' said Ben.

'Maybe my Dad or something. Something fucked-up happened at their house and I think I was drugged,' I said, my voice weakening.

'That's a lot of ifs,' Austin said. 'I may not be a favourite person where your Dad's concerned, but he's a good guy and that company makes good money. You need to sort it out, bruv!'

I sat feeling ashamed in the small, smokey room, wondering how I had got into a position where Austin was telling me advice. He was right, though, and the thought of sorting out the mess was almost too much to bear. The thick, coarse scotch could barely stop my nerves from jangling.

'If you want, mate, we can go round there and do the business on 'em,' said Ben nonchalantly.

I turned and saw at a clearly angered but helpful friend staring back at me with compassion, something I hadn't experienced for a long time. These people, my friends, may have had their problems and defects, but they were still human. More human than any of the people I'd had the misfortune of knowing during my nightmare year. Despite the simple-minded act of violence a la carte, I was touched by the offer.

'Austin, can I borrow your bedroom and get some sleep?' I asked. 'I need to just stop for a minute.'

'Of course you can, but have a fucking shower first, mate!' he replied.

The 'shower' comment irritated me and sucked away at my ego a little. The tides of bad memories and squalor I had accumulated through festering amongst the negatives of my life had ceased to exist for a moment, and I had to let the comment fly. I got up from the table and left for the bedroom, feeling safety and closure wash over my beaten head.

As I left the room, Austin moved my luggage over to an empty, dusty area by the sofa, dumping it down onto the dirty wooden floor. Inside the case, a miniscule lone cufflink, alien to me and packed by Winston, jumped further down amongst the clothes, its hidden electrical components sending waves of audio to a distant receiver. Over the next few hours, my friends continued their conversation, unaware of the miniature invasion of our private gathering, seeping all possibilities of action to anonymous persons.

★ ★ ★

'What do you mean, he's left?' Anthony barked down a poor quality phone line.

'He cottoned on to it, somehow,' Julian said feebly.

'No! You fucked it up, you stupid sodomite,' shouted Anthony.

'Listen, there's no need to…' Julian retorted, but was immediately cut off.

'Don't fucking say nothing, prick,' replied Anthony. 'You finish this off and get me my money or they'll be no money for any of us! However, you will get a pair of dashing plastic bags filled with your blood tied around your scrawny fucking neck, with your own cock shoved in your mouth.'

Anthony moved a small bundle of betting chips on the table. A group of middle-aged men sat around a green poker table, their bloated faces and awful summer shirts creating a vector of bad taste. None of the men had so much as blinked while listening to the conversation; instead, they were taking bored sips from heavy crystal glasses filled with the very finest whisky.

'We chucked something in his suitcase and we can hear him and some people saying they're gonna come round for us,' Julian said.

'Well, deal with it, faggot!' Anthony clicked his phone together, ending the conversation.

★ ★ ★

The air was frozen with fear and any sign of strength had evaporated out of the window. Winston and Michael both looked towards Julian for a positive sign of direction, despite the realisation that the fierce barking down the phone was not a good one.

'It's not an exact science, you know,' Winston moaned. 'It worked, you all saw it work. But not everyone behaves exactly how you want them to.'

'I don't fucking care, you imbecile. He was supposed to be meek and mild! We got the info we needed for the cash and all I asked was that he be kept in the dark,' Julian shouted as he edged closer to Winston. 'How did he get any idea of what was going on?' he continued. 'The answer is sloppiness! Fuck-ups because of too much drugs, too much laziness.' His face was now touching Winston's.

Without being seen, Julian pulled a small sharp knife from inside the crevice of the sofa while eyeballing Winston. He tightened his grip around the blade so tightly that his knuckles whitened and almost cracked.

'I've worked as a hypnotherapist. I've never tried to get a negative effect with this type of thing,' Winston said, his voice cracking like a teenager.

The knife was plunged into Winston's leg with a

sudden twitch of the hand. Winston tilted his head back, facing the ceiling, without emitting a sound for several seconds, his mouth wide open. Then he emitted a high-pitched screaming roar of pain, while a bloody writhing hand raced towards his mouth to cover the curdling sounds. As Winston silenced his own screams, like a guilty masochist, Julian twisted the knife again, causing a violent wound that he knew would not close naturally. Winston's eyes shuddered and began to show burst blood vessels and constricted pupils, before he flopped against the sofa like a dead fish.

'Baby, is he going to be alright?' said Michael casually.

'Shut up Michael and get me the phone,' Julian shouted as he got up from the blood-soaked sofa.

'Why?' Michael whined.

'I am not gonna let some two-bit thugs come round here to sort us out. Who does he think he is, having friends like that?' Julian continued to ramble. 'Homophobic in this day and age! How pathetic!'

★ ★ ★

A loud knock smacked at the door and thundered into the recess of the flat. I woke up instantly and sat bolt upright on the bed. There was a further two loud knocks and I deduced from the sound that the visit was official and urgent, an experience gained from having police knocking at my door at unexpected moments.

'Police! Open the door!' ordered a deep cockney voice.

Austin dashed past my field of vision from the bedroom, his quick pace unusual and ferment. I got up from the bed and walked on tiptoes to the bedroom door, closing it quickly. Kneeling down, I put my head against the frame in order to listen to the outcome. I heard the front door open and Austin cough from the heightened adrenaline, almost punctuating the air with nervousness.

'Patrick!' Austin exhaled. 'I mean, Inspector Strangeways.'

'Planning a little visit anywhere, Austin?'

I move slightly to look through the keyhole of the door. Squinting, I can just make out what is happening.

The uniformed officers light up the dark communal hallway of the flat like traffic cones, and shuffle in their plastic clothing as they linger behind the superior officer, the sound of digital bleeps erupting from their equipment.

'Who's here?' the Inspector barked. 'We've just had a call from two concerned citizens that you've threatened to attack them.'

'I've done no such thing,' Austin replied.

'That young lady's been filling us in on some more evidence as well,' the Inspector continued, leaning in to eyeball Austin. 'It could make things a lot worse for you if you start lying to me.'

Austin glanced at the closed bedroom door and kept his head low, avoiding eye contact.

'We both know you can't come in without a warrant,' he quips bravely.

The officer screwed his face up tight, biting his lip at the very edge, while the two brightly-coloured coppers looked blankly at each other. The officer leaned in close to Austin's face, as if smelling his sweaty skin.

'Don't say I didn't warn you!' he hissed.

With that, the three men walked away, trenching down the stairwell with pace, leaving Austin to close the door and face the music. As the door clicked shut, I came slowly out from the bedroom and stood in the doorframe.

'You owe me big time for this,' said Austin.

'I know I do!' I said humbly, looking down at the floor.

With his dirty clothes and bad habits, Austin was a product of his own misery. As he walked past me into the living room, I could see his dull tired eyes reflect the light, causing him to wince and cough like an elderly man who's smoked his entire life. He had come from good stock and was isolated from his family, including three older brothers who held jobs and had kids, who were still invited round to his mother's at Christmas. His Anglo-French upbringing meant he had travelled and been educated well; he was bi-lingual and boasted a high IQ, taking his father's ingenuity and his mother's artistic temperament. It was the death of his father at sixteen that split the man in half, living a normal life like so many others, yet also with a foot in the criminal underworld.

Like most offenders who don't want to be living the criminal life, but do it anyway to spite the world, he got caught, got lazy and gave up. He was walking his own green mile.

★ ★ ★

Anthony touched down from a long haul flight at Heathrow Airport at precisely 7.03 am. The thick fog and cold, biting frost was in sharp contrast to the blistering sunshine he had left only twelve hours earlier. At 10.12

am, Anthony arrived unannounced outside Julian and Michael's apartment in the East End of London, unwelcome and extremely jet-lagged.

His hired goon followed just feet behind him as he stomped in £200 shoes up a flight of steps towards the entrance. As he stood aside to allow the other man to pry open the middle lock, he watched as the vapour particles left his cracked lips.

Inside, Winston was lying on the couch, asleep. His face, pale from blood loss, was milky under the reflection of the miserable light streaming through the window.

'You going to wake up and make us some coffee?' said Anthony loudly, standing directly above Winston.

Winston woke up slowly in response to Anthony's voice. However, before he had time to react, the anonymous helper picked up an orange that was sitting on the table and shoved it into Winston's mouth. Winston immediately began to splutter, using his hands to fight the man off, before letting the fruit rest inside his mouth, eyes wide open and fearful. He held his hands out in front of him, in an attempt to deflect any further violence.

'Oh yeah!' said Anthony. 'Your hands are free. Suppose we'll have to leave the gagging til later.'

There was a pause as the two men stared down at Winston as he attempted to remove the orange from his mouth.

'Perhaps not. Maybe I could have another go?' said Anthony, as he grabbed Winston's hand.

'What do you want?' Winston managed to say, trembling with fear.

'It's simple, really,' replied Anthony. 'You have codes, passwords and things I need to get my money. You can tell us where it is.' He sat down on the edge of the coffee table, alongside Winston. 'It will play out like this. My partner here will leave the oranges where they are and you will clean this horrible mess up after we leave the house. And it *is* a horrible mess. I thought gay people were meant to be clean, but look at all this crap.'

He turns his head to look around the room, but then spies the bandage around Winston's leg. He sits fixated on the wound, tilting his head as if admiring a piece of art.

'Your leg doesn't look too clever, either,' he said. 'We'll be taking your phones and cash as well, because I have gone to a lot of effort.'

Anthony looked directly at the terrified Winston, pointing a fat finger at his peaky forehead. The hired helper stands on in silence looking ever taller and fatter, his stony face staring down without any comprehension.

'You see, you're basically a parasite,' went on Anthony. 'You might think we are parasites, but at least were giving you a taste of what those who interact with you feel like every day. What we hope we won't do is permanently attach you to that couch. Now, Winston, is there something you would like to tell us?'

'In the bedroom! Lift the bed up,' Winston spat out. 'The bed springs back into the wall, you'll be able to pull open a draw on the opposite side. Everything is there. Jesus, can't we work something out?'

The hired goon walked out the room and, after a terrifying thirty seconds with Anthony eyeballing Winston through pinned pupils, he returned into the living room with a blue plastic box filled with drugs, money and various gadgets. The goon lowered the box down between the two men and Winston nervously put his hand in the box, dried blood still staining his thumb and forefinger, and slowly held up a USB stick.

'It's loaded!' Winston said. 'Everything you need.'

The goon snatched the small object out of Winston's hand, allowing him to lower his tired arm. He looked on as the hired helper emptied cash and drugs into his leather jacket, while Anthony appeared unimpressed.

'Right, my friend. That's part one. Now all you have to do is give me your phone and your keys,' said Anthony with an outstretched palm.

'How do you know we don't have partners?' Winston asked bravely. 'They might find you and put you through ten tons of shit.'

Anthony looked back at the anonymous goon standing beside him and then nodded, before getting up and adjusting his jacket and trousers. As the two men begin walking towards the door, Winston turns his head to follow them.

'Because, my friend,' replied Anthony.

Winston listened to the men's footsteps on the wooden floors of the hallway, his heart pulsating horribly. He looked on at the window as the dull morning light poured down onto his face.

He caught sight of a knife held above his head, the metal blade shining under the reflection of the window. The sound of bursting liquid ticked off in his ears as the blade chopped through his neck and tore the carotid artery.

The rubbing of skin against icy cold metal was all he could feel. As blood sprayed out from his body and hit the window with force, the burly owner of the knife walked back out of the living room. Winston twitched with the last pumps of his heart, his eyes dull and lifeless.

★ ★ ★

Austin sat on his usual rickety chair nursing a cup of tea and listening intently to the story of Anthony, the debt and the plan. I could see he was listening, but it was very clear he had something to say the entire time I was talking.

'That man is what you would call a gangster,' he said. 'He's naturally violent and wealthy. His money is legal. He was making a ton of it in the late eighties and early nineties.' Austin took another sip of his tea, having shared his limited knowledge on the subject.

'Most of it's now in drugs and clubs,' piped up Ben from across the room. 'Intelligence is no match for natural stupidity. Anthony is the kind of man that you don't want to be in debt to, even if you're a friend of his!'

I sat back on the second-hand but comfortable sofa, minding my arm for dirty stains as I moved to get more comfortable. I felt that the room was working against me and I could sense the two men needed a little inspiration to push through my plot.

'Anthony might be tougher than a butcher's dog when he's barking,' I said, 'but he's weak underneath. He has a big problem with showing off.'

'Confession is good for the soul, but bad for your

career. That sort of thing?' Ben said, pulling another cigarette from a B&H box.

'Exactly,' I replied quickly and stood up. 'I know Anthony has a lock-up somewhere just outside East London, maybe Essex. It's his hub.'

'I don't think we need to know where his dildo collection is,' Austin sneered through a slurp of tea.

'Seriously now. I don't waste my time for the sake of it. This lock-up has everything. Drugs by the pound, cash, guns and deeds. We are talking millions. All locked away in a dirty, undesirable can in the middle of nowhere.'

'So, you're talking about robbing him and running?' said Ben, turning his head to look me in the eyes, as if waiting for a punch line.

'Fifty-fifty split,' I replied with a deadpan expression. 'You'll never have to work again. We get out the country before daybreak.' I scanned both their faces, trying to gauge their reaction.

Both of them looked away, refusing to make eye contact. The tense hope of persuading them to join me in my last-ditch selfish plans looked increasingly unlikely. I lit up a cigarette and waited for a response, the taste of tobacco thick and horrible in my mouth.

'How do we know this isn't going to fuck us up?' Ben said, blowing a fume of smoke across the musty room.

'How do you know this shit-fucking life won't kill us?' I responded angrily. 'You that happy doing this, day after day?'

Ben looked at me and said nothing, the thundering truth leaping out of my mouth and breaking down the air around us. Austin shuffled in his chair and then looked up at me slowly, the attention and closure that would decide our fate brewing and whistling around us.

★ ★ ★

Inside the South London police station, Inspector Patrick Strangeways sat in a dull grey office staring at a fake oak security door emblazoned with the blue Metropolitan Police badge. His suit clung around his waist, the large mid-day lunch busting his gut and forcing laziness between his eyes. He looked at a mobile phone that lay on the cheap table in front of him, waiting for an action.

The door buzzed and Julian walked in, slamming the door wide open with an open palm. Michael followed in small nervous steps, white and frail as a result of the commotion that life had become in such a short space of time. Without saying a word, they both sat down on the fixed plastic chairs and faced Patrick.

'Our friend is dead and the USB is gone,' began Julian. 'We walked into a bloodbath with the fucking voodoo man in the middle of it and came straight here.'

Silence was thick in the room. Patrick took his mobile off the table and clicked a few buttons, scanning the small screen. Julian lit up a cigarette, spying the 'No smoking' sign and exhaling a cloud of smoke in defiance.

'I'll have the mess taken care of, obviously,' he puffed away. 'Not that it's worth worrying about, right now. Dead bodies can be a hazard in my line of work.'

'Did you know that your buyer is here?' Patrick asked without looking up. 'Arrived today and seen at the airport.'

'What are we going to do?' Michael asked.

Patrick slammed his hands down on the table and stared daggers at Michael as if he was a putrid, dying rat. Julian remained unnerved.

'We are in a police station, in case you've forgotten!' Patrick barked at Michael. 'Hold yourself together.'

'You know that's not how it works!' Julian growled.

Julian swung his right arm violently over Michael and landed his hand on top of his forehead, the left arm coming up from behind at the back of the neck. For a moment it seemed to Patrick as if he was attempting to break Michael's neck.

'Sleepem,' Julian whispered in a soothing tone into Michael's right ear.

As Julian's hands slipped down and away, Michael flopped his head forward, eyes closed. Patrick sat, astonished at the vacant body. It seemed to him as though Michael was in a deep hypnotic state.

Julian pulled out a small battery-sized device from his jacket pocket and slid it across the table, the headphones still attached.

'I think they are going to rob his lockup,' Julian said quietly. 'We heard them talking about going balls out and taking him for everything.'

Patrick took the recording device slowly into his hands, placing one headphone into his ear and then started the media file. Julian sat frozen in his chair, the stark cold room reminding him of how close to the knife edge they really were. When the file came to an end, Patrick disconnected himself from the headset and slid the phone over to Julian.

'You ring him and tell him,' Patrick spoke through

gritted teeth. 'Don't hold back. And hope...' he paused. 'For all our sakes.'

'The only thing you're worried about is how hard my people will come down on you if certain activities come to light.' Julian stood up slowly and leant over the desk.

Patrick looked uncomfortable and squirmed in his seat.

'You had one purpose,' Julian continued menacingly. 'To keep an eye on our subject and the rats that follow. You are a dirty cop who should be protecting people and serving the law.' Julian lowered his voice to a whisper. 'But you're not, because you like money and you're lazy!'

Julian walked around the table and stooped down to face Patrick from the side, his breath touching the Inspector's capillary-red cheeks.

'This has been going on for two years now. Although I will admit that the subject has delivered us to all sorts of targets, this has got to end.'

★ ★ ★

Ben and I stood in the middle of a forest in Epson, the darkness of night and the winter air providing a cushion of space between us and the rest of the world. Ben pulled out a rusty Glock semi-automatic handgun with tape wrapped around the base. It looked old and unreliable, and it rattled in his hand.

'Do you know what you're doing with that?' I asked. 'And, may I ask, where exactly did these guns come from?'

'Look, I got the guns from a good connection. He did me a good deal on them as well.' Ben pointed the gun at a tree, squinting his eye as he did so.

I quickly put my hand over the top of the weapon and looked at him with anger, the signal to behave and be quiet.

'It's not loaded yet, for fuck's sake,' he said.

'A really good deal?' I said. 'A good connection? Bought from a bloke in a betting shop or a back alley of some sort?' My sarcasm washed over him.

'Look, I know you said use replicas,' replied Ben, holding his hands in the air. A glint from the gun caught my eye in the darkness. 'It's just for emergencies.'

'Carrying a gun around ain't gonna look good if the police do a random search,' I said. 'The likelihood of which is pretty high with a bent copper on our tail.' I turned my back to him and clenched my teeth in frustration.

Ben pulled a face in contempt and his fingers squeezed around the gun with frustration, his plans going up in smoke. He took the safety clip off with a small 'click' and snapped his arm upright, pulling the trigger and firing off a round with an almighty bang. I twisted around in a flash and I could see him smiling at the smoking barrel.

'What the fuck?' I shouted.

He moved his head with a tilt in the direction of the gun and pointed with his free hand towards the tree. As I looked, I could see a dead squirrel soaked in blood, lying at the bottom of the tree, its twisted body releasing guts into the undergrowth. My horror and ill-feeling towards Ben kept me transfixed on the poor deceased animal as my human counterpart fiddled with the machinery in his hand.

'Look, we are hardly Al Qaeda, so we won't get

searched!' Ben exclaimed. 'Bent copper or not, we're doing a robbery not a cake sale.'

We stared at each other in silence as the wind howled down through the bare trees, dead leaves swooping past our feet, creating a cacophony of noise around us.

'How did you get to be friends with those idiots Julian and Michael?' said Ben suddenly.

I chose not to answer him, but the question remained in my head. I had met them some two years earlier, but I couldn't actually remember the circumstances. I continued to ignore him and thought hard, almost sending myself into a trance while trying to remember when I had first met the two men, biting my lip hard until it bled.

★ ★ ★

My family home was set in the middle of a quiet street in a suburban town. The only sounds that you could hear during the day were our neighbours and their brood walking up and down the streets between school hours. The air was foggy and cold, making even the smallest trip outside an unpleasant and forgettable journey.

Austin walked down the road towards my parents' house dressed in a woolly hat, gloves, thick hiking jacket and hiking boots. The only part of him that was visible was the pale, lower half of his face, the rest of his head being tilted forward as he walked briskly towards his target. As he approached the house, he fumbled inside his coat pocket and pulled out a golden door key wrapped on a small piece of string, my last remaining possession before

I left for Thailand, stolen from my jacket while I was in his bathroom.

He looked around furtively before opening the front door and letting himself in. He knew from the time and day of the week that my parents would be out and that he had hours before anyone might come home, knowledge he had previously accumulated from loose tongues. As he closed the door and pulled off his hat, his rat-like eyes jumped about in his putrid face, looking around him to get acclimatised. His mobile phone buzzed in his pocket and he pulled the phone out to read a text: '*Get on with it and get out of there – Patrick*'.

He entered the first door on his right, keeping his gloves on despite the change in temperature, causing him to sweat and itch. His nerves wreaked havoc on his damaged heart and lungs as he traipsed inside my parents' house. He could see our family dog curled up in its basket down by the end of the room, his sweet, innocent face looking up to greet the unwelcome guest.

'Come here boy,' Austin said as he clapped his thighs for attention.

Our dog had been in the family for nearly ten years. He was old and tired most days and slept like a champion, the smell of curry or Sunday roast dinners the only thing that would guarantee his presence in the dining room. We loved him like a brother, and my parents treated him like another son; he was an innocent and a wonderful being, who only gave out love and asked for the simplest of things to survive.

The psychopathic tendencies of Austin burst through the façade as he grabbed at my aged dog, using his other hand to muffle his barks and cries for help. As he wrestled with my dog and held him down by the neck, he pulled out a large-barrelled syringe from his jacket pocket, biting off the needle guard with his manky teeth. Without compassion or humility, Austin poisoned our family pet without a second thought. Not enough poison to kill outright, but just enough to fatally injure for a long, drawn-out death, so that my parents would arrive home to find a helpless, dying animal.

★ ★ ★

Ben and I wandered back though the dead leaves towards the car park at the edge of the forest. Silence and darkness were the only factors present apart from the rhythmic sound of crunching leaves. I could sense that something was wrong and, down to the very edge of my guts, a stabbing sensation tore at me, causing me to pull a very miserable face. Two double bleeps sounded from Ben's pocket and he pulled out a mobile phone, reading the text while we walked. He squinted his eyes and tried to read the text, but his uneven gait made it almost impossible to read.

I chose not to ask what the text read, the recent events of my life having promoted a sense of deep privacy for myself and for others. If I didn't need to know something, then I didn't want to be told.

'Can I borrow your phone?' I asked Ben.

'Okay mate,' Ben replied.

I took the phone from Ben and navigated my way through the unnecessarily difficult touch screen, and then tapped in my digits.

'I need to call my parents and let them know about the stolen data,' I said to Ben as I pressed the phone against my ear.

Ben didn't reply, but instead kept his eyes forward as I held on to the phone, listening to the connection tone. I become slightly nervous as the dialing tone continued; the cold air buzzed in and out of my mouth in quick bursts, while my eyes swivelled around frantically at nothing. The thought of speaking with my family filled me with dread, the tense self-disapproval making decent communication almost impossible. I knew that I had to warn them about the stolen data before any major harm was done, even if it was at the cost of an already damaged relationship.

'Hello,' my father said in a hollow tone.

'It's me,' I replied.

'Before you say anything I need to tell you something,' he said. There was a long pause before he continued. 'It's the dog.'

I could feel the depression and anxiety transfer down the phone to me in a second, the telepathic-like quality of family troubles transposing words. My heart began to thump again in a painful unbalanced pattern, something that had become familiar during the recent months.

'I'll come over,' I said forcefully.

★ ★ ★

It was the first time the whole family had been together in months, their gloomy faces a shock to see under the painful circumstances. We piled into my father's car as my brother held the dog in a blanket, his face a picture of abject misery and helplessness. No one was speaking and yet we had managed to organise the late night trip to the vet and coordination of the family with extreme ease, perhaps the stark tragic situation forcing us into a tightly-knit unit. The car radio was left off and each of us sat in the compact BMW in silence, holding back the strain of tears and agitation no matter what. I looked from the back seat of the car to our family dog and could see his wide, frightened eyes staring back at me for help. At that moment I would have swapped positions with him for anything, my sins so much greater in need of punishment than that of such a sweet animal.

We finally reached the vets and unloaded ourselves into the waiting room, silence the only measure still prevalent amongst my family. We knew he was going to die and there was nothing we could do, the other problems within our family taking a back seat against the painful events that were unfolding. After a short while, the young female veterinarian opened the pale blue door to where our dog was being examined and walked out with her head held down, the lack of light in the reception area making her entrance appear ethereal.

'Would you like to come in?' she said.

We walked in, one by one, only to see our beloved pet lying down on a cold metal slab under the harsh lighting. We fought back tears at the sight of his helpless face that we loved so much. My father stood behind us and remained as strong as possible, no tears or sounds to be heard as he supported the family at our time of need. The vet had already connected an injection point to the dog's paw and began to twist a small syringe to the tube, filled with a blue liquid, unnatural in colour and capacity.

He died quickly and painlessly, gently held down on his side while the injection was given; his tongue poked out from his mouth and lapped one last time before his kind, familiar eyes dilated. We cried quietly and felt a unity of pain, trying to remain as dignified as possible, as we walked away from a part of our family that we would never see again.

★ ★ ★

I met Ben outside Austin's apartment block shortly after being dropped off by my family on the way home from the vets. He was standing outside the door casually smoking a cigarette in the freezing cold, looking at me with a blank expression, the apparent lack of knowledge emphasised in his forced demeanour. The streets were empty and quiet and my anger was building inside me, pulsating with malevolence.

As I burst through the door of the flat, with Ben a few paces behind me, I could see Austin sitting in silence on his sofa smoking a cigarette, ignoring my presence. I immediately sensed that something was wrong.

'What's wrong with you?' I asked.

He pulled on the cigarette and breathed out smoke from his mouth and nose at the same time, giving him valuable seconds in which to ignore me a little further.

'It's been a long day and a long night,' he snarled through the smoke.

I sat down beside him on the sofa and looked out at the same wall staring at nothing in particular.

'It's been a much harder day for me,' I replied.

I turned my head towards him, looking at the two-day-old stubble and pot marks on his slightly swollen face, his hand shaking as he held the cigarette.

'I'm sure,' he replied in a vengeful tone.

We sat in further silence as Ben sat on one of the wooden chairs by the coffee table, one of the legs wobbling from a half-broken fixing. I continued to watch Austin before turning to look at Ben, noticing the vacant look on his face, making no movement at all. I knew that something was wrong and the air around us sat as awkwardly as the two men. It was almost as if they wanted me to twig a difficult situation, one which I would inadvertently connect with.

'My dog died today,' I said suddenly. 'It was the first time I'd seen my family in a long while.' I paused and looked at each of the men; they refused to look back at me.

'Here, have a pipe!' Ben replied casually.

The pipe was lined with cocaine. Ben passed it over with trembling hands.

'I'm not sure I want it,' I said half-heartedly.

However, I put aside my moral sense of dignity and reached out towards the small metal pipe, a twinge of guilt making me sigh with disappointment. I lit the gauze and watched the chemical melt and frazzle as the smoke entered my lungs, the dizzy euphoria of dopamine flooding my brain and heating my body like a furnace.

As I continued to inhale, I looked to my left and noticed scratch marks down Austin's right arm, similar to that of an animal's mark, while his cigarette was held loosely between slightly blood-stained fingers. I exhaled, the anxiety caused by connecting the injury to recent contact with an animal made me choke, drawing conclusions that should have been mere paranoia.

'Where did you get that scratch?' I asked.

Austin stubbed out his cigarette and leant back in the sofa, as if the question was insignificant.

'Mangy dog!' Austin replied.

I could feel my heart jump into my mouth and a series of desperate thoughts flooded my brain. I wondered how he could make such an insensitive comment. I felt hostility in the room and I knew that I was the source, waves of anger and violent possibilities entering my head and excreting from my every pore.

'Did you?' I asked quietly, my blood pumping like a locomotive.

The two men ignored me. I stood up from the sofa and stared down at Austin as if he were vermin. He slowly angled his head towards me with a small, nasty smile and a twinkle of excitement in his eyes. All my worst fears and hunches about the man that I'd chosen to ignore over the years suddenly became an all too unbearable reality.

I grabbed at his jacket with both hands, clenching my firsts around the material, hoping to reach his skin and cause some pain. Lifting him up to his feet with ease, I threw him against the dirty yellow wall.

'You psychopath!' I shouted in his face. 'You killed my dog?'

I clenched my hand behind me, feeling the adrenaline line my muscles with venom and power, before crunching an almighty blow against his jaw, the snap and crash of the hit spewing blood from his cracked lips.

As I readied for myself for another shot at him, Ben slid close to me with a used syringe filled with blue liquid and slid it into my jacket pocket before clamping his arms around me and attempting to pull me off. However, the anger within me was too great and I threw him back with a shove of my body.

'Take him to the police!' Ben shouted at Austin, 'Don't do what he wants.'

I readied myself for another shot, but Ben's comment made me see the logic and a stronger sense of justice began to take effect in my mind. I slowly lowered my arm, my gritted teeth still spitting saliva and hot breath, and eyeballed Austin with disgust and horror.

'Okay, I will!' I said aggressively before spitting in Austin's face. 'Let's do the right thing.'

I stepped back from Austin, releasing my grip. All three of us stood in the room, regaining our breath, while the still smoking pipe lay on the floor, filling the room with the bitter smell of cocaine and old metal.

* * *

Having dragged Austin round to the local police station, with Ben staggering behind us the entire way, I released my hidden hand, which held a short four-inch blade against the side of his jacket. I faked a smile, overacting and talking rapidly, fuelled by extreme hate and hyperactivity, pretending we were two pals heading home or on to the next club. I'd be lying if I said that a part of me didn't enjoy the control and energy inside me; perhaps it was the latent hatred of the years of drug use with the man spilling out into one night. I wanted to plunge the blade into him, but the fact that my beloved pet had died, had been murdered, made me control the hunger for blood.

As we walked into the modern police station, we were greeted at the top of a rising sloped entrance by a familiar face. Patrick, the dirty bastard cop, was standing between us and the reception wearing a baggy white shirt and an old polyester tie, hands on hips, as if he was the Sheriff of Nottingham.

'What's going on here?' Patrick asked.

'I'm bringing in this piece of filth!' I shouted. 'He murdered my family dog earlier today.'

'That's an odd and intriguing claim,' he replied.

'Why?' I said angrily.

'Well, we've had calls saying that, in fact, you are off your head and out of control. That, actually, we should pull *you* in before someone gets hurt.'

'Bollocks! You know I wouldn't come here without a reason.'

'Do you know it's against the law to force someone against their will, like you're doing?'

'How do you know I've forced him?'

The dirty cop walked down to me and stood very close, wearing an annoying smirk that I wanted to wipe clean off his face. He put his hand inside my left coat pocket and pulled out a 5ml syringe, still filled with a small amount of blue liquid, which he held up to the light to examine.

'Sure it wasn't you?' he asked me.

I started to laugh and continued the forced charade of comedy, knowing full well that I'd been set up. Patrick and the others looked at me as I continued to laugh; I even crouched down a little, holding my knees, as if totally amused, when in actual fact I was losing my balance, the fear and surprise almost knocking me over.

'I've already been on the phone to your parents,' Patrick said with implausible softness. 'We are going to get you some help.'

I stopped laughing at once and straightened up to look him. The realisation of what he really meant made me want to vomit in his face.

'You're going to get me sectioned.'

I started to laugh again and held on to the disabled access bar beside me, looking behind and around me to see if I had a clear shot of escaping, but two uniformed officers were already standing behind me.

'It's best, it really is!' Patrick said with implied force.

* * *

Patrick walked down to the East London sauna dressed in a long, dark overcoat and an old, mothballed baseball cap. The smile hidden under the hat and collar spread across his face as he thought about his recent successes and the fact that no one knew about this 'secret pastime'. He sent a message from his phone to his wife, just as he passed underneath the faux Greek pillar entrance.

Changed and wearing a lengthy towel and flip-flops, he headed up to the club's facilities. He passed through the CCTV cameras and entered through a cabin door, where a strung-out Michael was waiting nervously.

'Well, I've got an hour and it's time to celebrate,' said Patrick.

'Good for you,' Michael chirped back sarcastically.

Outside the main entrance, an angry middle-aged woman was smoking a cigarette and letting the spitting rain ruin her hair. She stamped out the cigarette with an expensive high-heeled shoe and plastered a fake smile across her face, the lines and tendons struggling to maintain the position. As she entered the sauna, she beamed at the receptionist.

'Hello darling, sorry to bother you,' she said in a posh London accent, 'but I am bursting for a pee. Could I use your facilities?'

The receptionist looked puzzled.

'Well, I'm not supposed to, you know,' he eventually replied in a Latin accent.

'It's raining outside and I live on the other side of London,' she continued, clasping her wet hair.

The receptionist pointed to a door on the right and buzzed her in, before explaining that the toilets were just up a small flight of stairs.

'Please just use this toilet and stay out of sight,' he said. 'The rules are strict, my darling.'

The woman walked up the stairs and blew a kiss in appreciation, the tap of her heels clicking on the stairs. Once she reached the top of the stairs, she looked around for another door and found one marked 'Employees Only' and scurried through quietly. Inside the small room was a ton of cleaning equipment, the smell of bleach making her eyes water. She spied a second door on the other side and ran through it. It brought her to a communal pool area where men were lying around on deck chairs and swimming. The sight of her caused swift alarm.

Out of her pocket she pulled a switchblade and sparked it open, grinding her teeth in anger as she stomped through the communal area unhindered, looking left and right for her victim. She took a left at the end of the room into the cabin area and pulled open a door revealing two men performing a sex act. She closed the door in shock.

Regaining her perspective, she suddenly heard a man's voice followed by a familiar laugh. She followed the sound to the end of the corridor, passing through CCTV cameras, and stood outside the door. With a deep breath, she pulled open the door and saw her husband sleazing over another man, the sight of which caused her to freeze.

'What the fuck are you doing here?' said Patrick, mortified.

'Someone told me you'd be here,' his wife replied, her voice breaking.

The two men froze and stared at her. Just then, Michael noticed the blade in the woman's shaking hand. When her eyes connected with Michael's and realised he had seen the knife, she suddenly tore forward like a bear, slashing awkwardly at Michael's neck. Blood began to pour from the carotid artery, instantly and dramatically.

As Patrick stepped in to apprehend her, she pulled the blade from Michael's neck and slashed it back into the abdomen of her husband. As Patrick fell forward onto the floor, the impact pushed the knife deeper inside his solar plexus, piercing his spine from the front and killing him instantly. The woman turned and ran away like a frightened girl, holding her sobs through a bloody hand as she made haste from the bodies.

★ ★ ★

My father stood in the freezing cold by the River Thames, next to an old brown bench, taking in the view of the grey, wintry afternoon. He pulled his mobile phone from his pocket and checked the screen for a message or update, anxious to complete this meeting. Anthony and Julian strolled up behind him quietly, wearing equally dull grey suits, the sound of swans and wind piercing the ice-cold air. They both approached the left side of the bench and sat down, giving my father space on the right side, without the need for fusty, useless words.

'I am sorry we have ended up in this predicament,' Julian began.

'Well, it is what it is!' my father snapped. 'He is incarcerated and there's nothing anyone can do about that.'

'I can only tell you that he has gone round the bend,' Anthony quipped. 'I would have said something sooner, before my friend here showed me something else.'

'Well, what is it?' my father snapped again. 'What could possibly make this any worse?'

'Video footage of him, that we have, makes it *much* worse,' said Julian.

Julian pulled out a large android phone and began to access video files, while Anthony leaned over slightly to catch my father's eye. The short stare between them is one of mutual mistrust, but Anthony managed a wrought smile. Julian passed the phone to my father's cold hand, already playing the video file, and he squinted to make out the high resolution image on the screen.

On the screen, a voice asks a direct, clearly audible

188

question and I reply succinctly, each answer separated by editing. I am visible to the camera, sitting on a small single bed against a wall, looking inebriated and tired, my lips smacking together with dehydration between every word.

'Have you ever killed anyone?' the voice asked.

A long pause plays out on the video and the static increases, the rumbling of the handset coursing down into my father's hand.

'Yes.' I pause. 'Many.'

'Can you tell us the details?'

'Yes,' I answer robotically.

As the words sink out of the tiny speaker, my father reels at what he is being shown; his mouth slowly opens and he struggles to take a quiet inward breath. Anthony and Julian looked at each other and shared an unspoken message, while my father's heart beats in staccato rhythm, the symptoms of a panic attack beginning to take hold.

'Now, I want you to know that I did this as a favour for you,' Anthony said. 'My mates in the force are finally proving useful.'

Julian gave Anthony a sullied look and cocked his head to one side, which Anthony ignored and continued to look at my father's disappointed face.

'I have a suggestion to make,' said Anthony. 'If you agree, then everything will work out alright. Let's take a walk and I'll tell you all about it.'

★ ★ ★

The high-security mental health ward was aptly named 'Clover', after the supposed lucky clover in Irish heritage.

The facility, although large and costly, could hold only a few patients at a time, maybe five or six at the very most. The rooms, and even corridors, were designed to make it impossible to cause accidental harm, similar to a padded room stretching over an acre or so. If you wanted a piece of toast you would have to ask a member of staff to make it, while being allowed into the enclosed garden for a cigarette was an even bigger challenge. The place was quiet and bleak, blue and grey the only colours permitted, a TV encased behind bulletproof plastic being the only form of entertainment.

'When can I get out of here?' I said to my doctor.

'This is a max security ward,' the doctor replied. 'You have been accepted here under the observation that you are suffering from psychosis.'

The office we were sitting in was small, humid and cramped. The doctor's nylon grey suit and awful haircut made me uneasy, the thought of such cheapness perhaps affecting his sense of recognition. Perhaps, I wondered, my own sense of pride was misplaced.

'You know that you shouldn't be here, technically,' the doctor explained, 'but you have to prove that.'

'What does that mean?' I asked.

'Well, you have to turn down drugs and behave in an exemplary fashion.'

The meeting ended and I realised that, if I wanted to get out of this place, I had to behave like the most sensible, well-behaved person imaginable. I contacted my lawyer on the communal phone and discussed my options.

'You have to follow the doctor's advice. Meanwhile, I will file a wrongful section, which will hopefully get approved sooner rather than later,' was his only advice.

I spent the next week counting down every hour and managing only two hours sleep each night. The screams and inaudible tantrums from the unfortunate souls who suffered within the hospital wing made me feel a compassion that put my own problems into perspective.

★ ★ ★

One week later…

Julian, dressed in body armour and a smartly-dressed shirt and trousers, is sitting in the marked police car roaring towards the North, where a suspected killer was on the loose, causing a media mayhem. He sat next to a uniformed police officer who was driving the car at speed with a wailing siren. He sat bored out of his mind, waiting for the arrival.

'The guy has been missing for two days and has killed two people already,' the officer said. 'We'll hopefully will find him tonight at this river spot and seize him.'

'Well, officer, you need to take it as it comes!' Julian continued. 'If we do we do, and if we don't we don't.'

They drove in silence for another fifty miles, the roar of the armoured BMW providing the only background entertainment. Rothbury, Northumbria, on a Friday night, was going to be a bleak one.

They approached a cross section of the motorway opposing a large roundabout near the site and sat waiting, while the commuters whizzed round in front of them.

'You ever killed anyone, officer?' Julian asked.

'No sir!' the officer replied.

They continued to sit. A man then jumped out of the driver's side of his vehicle from behind the patrol car and sauntered up towards them. Julian could see the man in the mirror and noticed the huge physique and stature, dressed in a yellow t-shirt and jeans. Julian decided not to alert the other officer and continued to look in his side mirror at the man until he was alongside the passenger window. Julian looked face to face through the window at the angry-looking man. The man raised a sawn-off shotgun up towards Julian's face and rested the barrel on his left forearm. The gun blew shattered fragments at the car and took out the side of Julian's face. The impact sent fragments across to the uniformed driver amongst gasps of shock.

As blood dripped and spurted from the dead man's face and neck, the uniformed officer sat shaking in his driver's seat, trying to regain his breath.

The cold, dead eyes of Julian sat still and pinned, dripped in secondhand blood from the massive head.

★ ★ ★

I sat by the old-fashioned grey payphone in the desolate ward trying to ring my family, listening to the rings, one after the other, like nails sealing my miserable fate. I could feel the world changing around me every day despite my incarceration, while an eerie calm had become my new motto in place of the chemical assistance, like a Buddhist monk in a chemotherapy ward. This was very new for me and maybe it was good; the challenge, the chance to recover and be isolated. I did, however, wish to speak with my family more than I ever had and the lack of communication made me feel terrified and alone.

I walked back, dejected, from the phone and headed towards the security guard, who managed the garden door. He buzzed me out so I could light up yet another cigarette in the drizzling rain, wandering round the garden like one of the other inmates. They may have been miserable, but they certainly weren't sober; then again, nothing comes for free in this life.

I headed over to a young woman named Stacey and sat under the plastic shelter with her while we smoked. She suffered from extreme bouts of schizophrenia and had, as she'd described it, 'thirteen different voices in me 'ead'. I felt sorry for her and noticed that she looked like a normal, beautiful young woman and couldn't imagine what that torment must be like.

'I have this one voice in my head called "wanker" and I think he's trying to rape my sister,' she said in a frightened voice.

I remained silent, absorbed in shock, and smoked my cigarette. I noticed that the guards and nurses were watching us both closely. The rain drizzled on my shoes, but I didn't care. I looked up at the thirty-foot high fences that could be electrified with a switch. I wondered if I could tie my bed sheets together and hide them under a jacket as a means of an emergency escape; the desire to leave the place made me feel strong enough to do anything. It's funny how you can suddenly become so determined and strong when you have your dignity and freedom taken away.

* * *

Austin looked out from his living room window onto the street and sparked up a cigarette. He noticed the large amounts of courier vans shuffling near my family office and the presence of a dejected-looking brother and father standing in the doorway, looking pensive and angry. The fact that so many of his acquaintances had been found dead recently scared him to the point of making him pop nearly a box of Valium tablets a day, on top of his regular boat-load of smack and methadone juice. He still wasn't sleeping properly, and the large amount of cash that he had at his disposal to spend on crack cocaine and hookers, and whatever else he fancied, stayed firmly hidden. There was no way that he could enjoy himself at the moment; he wanted to sleep, untroubled, enclosed by the darkness.

Ben, being a younger and less thoughtful person, sat on the dirty sofa dressed in three-day-old underwear and a food-stained Metallica t-shirt, smoking copious amounts of rock cocaine and injecting ten bags of smack every few hours. He would have ordered prostitutes quite happily, but his cock was as much use as a banjo to a monkey. The thing about drug oblivion is that you become so relaxed and stupid that you just couldn't give a shit.

The door suddenly smashed open from the hallway and Austin buckled at the knees, feeling his heart cramp up. Ben turned his stoned head to the side, just in time to see the men dressed in masks and surgical gloves entering the flat with large, serrated knives. They wore plastic bags taped to their feet and crunched there way forward. One of the burly men stuck a blade into Ben's chest, twisted it and pulled out.

'Huuugh!' was Ben's final sound as they headed over to Austin.

'Please don't! You got the wrong man!' cried Austin hysterically.

The second heavy-set man stuck the blade into Austin's chest and pounded the end of the knife with his fist, severing the tissue of the heart. As the air gasped from Austin's mouth, a spurt of blood chocked out of his throat and hit the mask that hid the killer's face.

As the men left the building, extracting their protection from feet and faces, the victims lay strewn in the filthy, drug den apartment. The clump of dirty cash under Austin's bed would now never be used by anyone.

★ ★ ★

I left the hospital after nearly two weeks of incarceration and, with the help of an overweight and bumbling solicitor, I managed to have my sectioning withdrawn. I had refused all meds at all times, been the most polite, compliant person I could and even struck up bonds with most of the nurses. If I hadn't been labelled as a mental health patient I firmly believe I would have had a chance with one of them romantically, but the stigma and possible loss of job for her was a big fat blockade.

The taxi ride home was the most amazing feeling and experience. I felt euphoric and ready for anything, but kept my excitement in check; I remembered the cockiness I felt when I left Thailand and I didn't want a desperate repeat of that disaster. I watched the streets and people and open shops and felt so relaxed and optimistic, even chatting happily to my driver as if he was my long-lost best friend. It was amazing and I wanted to appreciate every second.

I arrived at my family's business office and paid the man his money, thanking him in an over-the-top way and tipping generously. I strolled up to the dark blue Victorian door and pressed the buzzer for the office, letting it ring while I prepared to show the healthy, happy me and to explain what I could. I'd decided that, even if they didn't want to hear much from me, I would just give them a hug and make the most of it. It would have meant the world to me.

No answer came from the buzzer and I looked up to the windows, but saw there were no lights on. In fact, the whole building seemed strangely quiet with no lights from any of the windows, which was highly unusual. I didn't want to form any conclusions and remained optimistic as I made my way a mile down the road to the family house, hoping to catch someone there. During the walk home, with the smile plastered on my face, I began to feel that maybe I *was* capable and strong, that I *could* make better decisions and be loved by people and love them back the way they deserved.

People stared at me as I walked, looking at the smile, which is what people always do when they see a lone person walking and looking happy in London. It didn't bother me because I wanted this to be the first day of my new life; exercise, healthy food, patience and sleep and, more importantly, the memory of my incarceration forcing me to feel strong. The biting wind in my face had no effect on me.

When I arrived home and strolled up to the front door, I noticed there was no car in the drive and the curtains had been drawn shut, upstairs and downstairs. There was no light seeping through and even the bins were together against the side wall, completely empty. A neighbour from next door walked out of her house and headed over to me. She was a young woman and looked smart and attractive; the face, however, was worried, but it seemed more of a temporary look, one she wasn't used to.

'They're gone I'm afraid, my darling,' she said in an eloquent, soft voice.

'Where? Why?' I asked.

'Big problems involving, from what I can gather, police and work, and even their own protection,' she said whilst looking down at her feet.

'When?' I said, suddenly feeling weak.

'I saw your Mother and Father drive off early one morning with the car packed. They gave me this.' She handed a note to me.

I sat down on the low bricked wall and opened the handwritten letter, seeing a lengthy explanation in my Mother's slanted writing. I began to read the contents slowly, my heart jumping painfully in my chest with sorrow and expectancy.

★ ★ ★

As I approached the river banks, located half a mile away from the family home, I used the side of my hand to wipe away my watering, tired eyes. The wind picked up and pushed against my body as I walked south to the freezing cold water, the dark green, thick Thames within sight. When I reached the water's edge, I sat down on a rotting brown bench, allowing the moisture to soak into the back of my jeans. The irritation of the dirty water reaching my skin through my clothing angered me and I clenched my teeth together, grinding the molars and tasting dust. A few people wandered past some way behind me, and I let myself stare into the murky water, the smell of the river disappearing into nothing.

I thought about walking into the river and holding myself under until I suffocated and drowned, the sewage and bacteria flowing inside my nostrils and into my brain. The thought caused me to push more anger to the surface of my mind and I washed away into more horrific dreams of slumber.

To be continued in Part Two